BEST MURDER IN SHOW

A SOPHIE SAYERS COZY MYSTERY

DEBBIE YOUNG

Boldwood

This edition published in Great Britain in 2022 by Boldwood Books Ltd. First published in 2017

Copyright © Debbie Young, 2017

Cover Design by Head Design Ltd

Cover Photography: Shutterstock

The moral right of Debbie Young to be identified as the author of this work has been asserted in accordance with the Copyright, Designs and Patents Act 1988.

Every effort has been made to obtain the necessary permissions with reference to copyright material, both illustrative and quoted. We apologise for any omissions in this respect and will be pleased to make the appropriate acknowledgements in any future edition.

A CIP catalogue record for this book is available from the British Library.

Paperback ISBN 978-1-80483-056-7

Large Print ISBN 978-1-80483-057-4

Hardback ISBN 978-1-80483-059-8

Ebook ISBN 978-1-80483-055-0

Kindle ISBN 978-1-80483-054-3

Audio CD ISBN 978-1-80483-063-5

MP3 CD ISBN 978-1-80483-060-4

Digital audio download ISBN 978-1-80483-058-1

Boldwood Books Ltd
23 Bowerdean Street
London SW6 3TN
www.boldwoodbooks.com

To Orna Ross: friend, mentor, and inspiration

A woman must have money
    and a room of her own
    if she is to write fiction.

— VIRGINIA WOOLF

Live a life worth writing down.
    Then write it down.

— MAY SAYERS

PROLOGUE
NO HEAD FOR MURDER

From where I was sitting, Anne Boleyn and Catherine Howard seemed remarkably clean and fragrant considering they'd just had their heads cut off. On the humid summer breeze the astringent scent of lavender wafted towards me from the pretty posies that hung from the waistbands of each of Henry VIII's six wives.

The severed heads of Anne Boleyn and Catherine Howard, made of papier-mâché-covered balloons, lay neatly in front of them, smiling benignly in wicker log baskets. Sugar-pink cardboard necks, inserted into the tops of their Tudor dresses, rested on upended breezeblocks borrowed from the local builder. The queens' real heads were safely concealed beneath the built-up shoulders of their costumes. The necks of their dresses, topped off with starched ruffs, were stitched closed to complete the illusion of their recent execution.

To stop the headless queens wobbling around as their carnival float progressed up the High Street, they were wired to the safety rail that ran around the edge of the trailer. Henry VIII's other four wives sat upright and entire on low wooden thrones borrowed from the choir stall of the village church. The king basked on the larger bishop's seat raised on a dais at the tractor end of the float.

You couldn't blame Tom, the executioner, for looking pleased with his neat work. All the way up the High Street, he'd waved to the crowd as proudly as if he'd just won *MasterChef*. Two small children burst into terrified tears at the sight of the dark hooded figure. They were comforted only when he pulled up his knitted balaclava, to reveal that it was really just Ian, the village school's lollipop man.

Over on the Wendlebury Writers' float, we thought it better not to wave. Smiling and waving, royal style, would have been all wrong from serious 'Literary Heroes'. I was Virginia Woolf.

As we waited, restless, to hear the judges' verdict, I noticed the Wendlebury Players' director Rex, self-cast as Henry VIII, staring at me. I couldn't believe he could be so shameless, knowing his girlfriend, Dido, was in the crowd. From the moment I'd met him at one of the Players' rehearsals back in June, there was something about him that put me on my guard. Blushing angrily, I faced the other way, hoping to goodness that Dido didn't think there was anything going on between us.

As a diversionary tactic, I pretended to be riveted by the WI's Suffragette-themed float, parked on the other side of ours. It was an interesting spectacle. In front of a backdrop painted to resemble a London city street ran a row of large iron railings: plastic fencing spray-painted gunmetal grey. To these were chained half a dozen middle-aged ladies in hired *My Fair Lady* costumes. The one at the centre wore a large rosette saying 'Mrs Pankhurst' to clarify their theme. All six were adorned with the Suffragette movement's distinctive green, purple and white sashes, the kind now more usually associated with beauty queens. None of the chained protesters looked as if they'd recently been in prison on hunger strike.

What would Virginia Woolf have made of the Village Show? I wished I'd done a little more research before picking her as my Literary Hero. I should at least have read one of her books. I'd only chosen her to try to impress my new friends in the Wendlebury Writers, and to look clever in front of my new boss, Hector Munro, proprietor of the village bookshop. Now dressed as Homer, he was towing our float with his Land Rover.

But never mind Virginia Woolf, I was still unsure of what to make of the Village Show myself. Although when I was still at school I'd spent a fortnight here every summer holiday, staying with my Great Auntie May, my visits had never coincided with the Show. Returning to live here at the age of twenty-five, I'd assumed taking part in the carnival parade would be innocent fun, but now I was not so sure.

Masking the sharp scent of fresh hay that bordered the arena, a new aroma cut into my senses: flatulence from the executioner now standing with his back to me and Anne Boleyn. Lucky her to have her head inside her dress to keep out of that little cloud, I was thinking just as a loud crackle from the tannoy alerted us that the judges were about to announce the results of the float competition.

The broad Gloucestershire burr of Stanley Harding, Village Show Chairman, boomed, 'Congratulations to another fine field of entries for the carnival procession.' His commentary was well practised, this being his twenty-first show in that prestigious position. The post was passed on as if by birthright – he'd taken over the role uncontested from his father, and it was his grandfather's before that. This latter-day feudal system didn't seem to do anyone any harm, if the bustling crowd's obvious delight with the proceedings was anything to go by.

'Thank you all for the wonderful hard work that you've put in to making such a fabulous display. In reverse order, this year's prizes are as follows. In third place, the WI for their Mary Poppins float showing Mrs Banks and her Sister Suffragettes.'

There was a roar of applause, and shrieks of delight from the chained ladies who seemed unperturbed that their serious political statement had been misinterpreted as a Disney movie. The Suffragettes tried to hug each other, forgetting they were all chained to the railings, and succeeded only in wrenching their arms and shoulders and dislodging the iron-effect fence. That they remained constrained added to the crowd's enjoyment. No-one came forward with the padlock keys to release them, despite their cries for help.

'Cor, those ladies are a force to be reckoned with,' continued Stanley. 'You chaps had better watch your backs once they get loose.' He paused for dramatic effect. 'In second place, the Wendlebury Players, for King Rex and his harem. No, only joking, Dido – I mean Henry VIII and his Six Wives. I understand that will be the theme of their next drama production in November, and I'm sure we're all looking forward to enjoying that event. Except perhaps the two wives that get their heads chopped off.' He let out a roar at his own joke. 'I bet now we've seen our Ian dolled up like this, all you boy racers will drive a bit slower past the school when he's on lollipop duty.'

While Stanley waited for the cheering to die down, I surveyed the remaining floats, crossing my fingers that we'd be the lucky winners. Ours was by far the most cultured entry.

'And now, the moment you've all been waiting for: this year's first prize goes to the Gardening Club, and their army of Worzel Gummidges.'

The human scarecrows were unable to join in the rapturous applause because they were all tied to wooden crosses, looking as if they belonged to some extreme Christian religious cult in which neatness of dress was not a core value. Their tractor driver leapt down from his cab to sever the scarecrows' ropes with a perilously sharp pocketknife. As soon as they'd all been freed, they collected a large silver trophy from Stanley and made a beeline to the beer tent to fill it up, courtesy of their prize money. A couple of them had lit cigarettes dangling from their mouths before they even reached the tent, with no regard for the straw stuffing poking out from their costumes. Now there was an accident waiting to happen.

I was more disappointed than I'd expected that the Wendlebury Writers hadn't won a prize. I wondered whether the problem was our lack of a bondage theme, worryingly present in all the winning floats. Seeing my glum face, Louisa, as Agatha Christie, got up from her low Art Deco armchair and came over to pat me on the shoulder consolingly.

'Never mind, dear, we entertained the crowds, and that's what really matters – all working together to put on a good show. Let's all go and have a nice cream tea in the hall now. Did you know Agatha Christie's favourite drink was Devon cream? She had it served in a wineglass with her dinner.'

I wished I had known Virginia Woolf's preferred tipple so that I could have made an appropriate reply.

As I started to descend the steps from our trailer, I was stopped in my kitten-heeled tracks by a scream from the direction of the Wendlebury Players' float. A headless Catherine Howard, who had just released herself from the ties that bound her to the safety rail, was bending over Anne Boleyn, shaking her built-up shoulders. Catherine Howard's voice was muffled by the thick fabric of her dress, despite the gauze across the bodice that allowed her to see out.

'Oh, my God, Linda's passed out! Somebody fetch some water! Untie her at once and help me get her out of this wretched costume. Rex, I told you we'd be far too hot with our heads stuck inside these dresses for hours on end.'

Hector jumped down from his Land Rover, pulled an antique dagger from the belt of his toga and offered it to Rex. Joshua, my elderly neighbour who had been leading the parade, appeared at his side brandishing a rusting penknife. Meanwhile, Anne of Cleves untied the wires that had kept Anne Boleyn's body in position. From the craft stall, Carol, the village shopkeeper and wardrobe mistress to the Wendlebury Players, came running at as full a pelt as a fifty-year-old lady could manage, waving a pair of dressmaking scissors. The sudden profusion of deadly weapons about the place was alarming.

'Don't you damage that dress, Rex. That's got to last four evening performances and a matinee in November.'

Pushing Rex aside, Carol swiftly undid numerous poppers, zips and buttons that she'd sewn in lovingly while making the dress the week before and eased it down over the fake neck. Only then was she able to remove the cardboard to reveal Anne Boleyn's real head underneath.

'Look at the colour of Linda's face, she's boiling hot,' cried Catherine Howard, ripping her dress's neckline to allow her head to surface from beneath her ruff. 'She's absolutely covered in heat rash. She must have fainted.'

Ian laid down his axe and crouched, frowning, beside the still-kneeling motionless body of Anne Boleyn. With one arm around her shoulders, he lay two podgy fingers gently on her slender neck. He looked up at Rex, standing stony-faced beside him and fidgeting with his codpiece. Rex's elegant girlfriend Dido, incongruous in twenty-first century fashion, had draped herself consolingly about him.

I didn't need to hear Ian's verdict. I already knew Linda Absolom was dead.

1

READER, I LEFT HIM

Two months earlier, back in Germany, Damian had predicted that the village would be full of murders. Mad men and murderers, to be precise.

'Little villages like Wendlebury Barrow are rife with backbiting and intrigue,' he told me over breakfast one June day. This was one of many reasons he gave me not to abandon him to move to the cottage I'd just inherited from my great aunt. 'You'll be murdered in your bed,' he'd said, 'and no-one will be there to hear you scream. You'll be lonely living on your own. You'll miss me.'

He gave me every reason except the one I wanted to hear.

'But her legacy is offering me a chance I'd never have if I stayed here,' I told him, pouring us each some coffee from the pot and setting his mug down in front of him. 'I'll be free to write books, like I've always wanted to, living rent-free in Auntie May's cottage.'

As usual, he was dismissive of my ambitions. 'What, you think you'll absorb her success by osmosis? Pick up her talent just by sleeping in her bed? Sell your books on the back of sharing her surname?'

'I don't know, but at least I've got to try. It's what she would have wanted.'

'You don't have to go and live in some backwater to write. You can write here. You can write wherever you are.'

'In Wendlebury Barrow it will be peaceful. Conducive to my art.' I glared at the man snoring on my sofa, one of his freeloading friends from his travelling English language theatre group, Damian Drammaticas.

'Yes, far too peaceful, on your own, in the middle of nowhere, in a sleepy little village where nothing ever happens.'

'Sounds fine to me.'

'You're a fantasist.'

He threw his toast crust down on his plate, spreading crumbs across the table.

'Well, duh, I'm a writer. It goes with the territory.'

'You'll never make money from writing. No-one makes money from writing. Don't you know that?'

'I make a lot more money than you do.'

I picked up his crust and took a bite. It annoyed me to see him waste my food.

'Yes, as a teacher, not as a writer. Besides, you'll miss teaching at these fancy international schools, moving from one European city to another every academic year. It won't be half as interesting teaching in England.'

'I'm not going to teach. I'm going to write. My auntie May always says – used to say – there's money in books, and she should know.'

'Only if you use banknotes as bookmarks. Anyway, you'll still need to earn money to live on. You'll never find a job in a little village like that.'

He drained his coffee cup and left it in the sink unwashed. Then he turned to me, all smiles. 'I tell you what, why don't you just sell the cottage and keep the cash? Then you'll be able to invest in a better van for the theatre group. You could be our official patron.'

I was glad I'd never taken him to meet my great auntie May.

Damian pointed to himself as the final exhibit in his long list of excuses. 'Don't you know when you're well off?'

For a moment, I surveyed his Viking good looks, thick blond hair and piercing blue eyes above a sturdy frame. Once they'd been enough to sway my judgement. But no longer.

'I think I do,' I said quietly, and logged on to my laptop to book my flight from Frankfurt to London. It was a one-way ticket.

2

NO PLACE LIKE HOME

Although I secretly feared Damian's misgivings about Wendlebury Barrow might be true, I was looking forward to being on my own in Auntie May's cottage. Even without her legacy, I was ready to come back to England after four years of working abroad. But where home was, I wasn't sure. At the age of twenty-five, I didn't want to move back in with my parents, academics currently working in Inverness. May's cottage would give me the solitude I needed to get my act together, and to work out what that act might be.

The peace and quiet of village life must have been part of Wendlebury's appeal to Auntie May. A dependable anchor in her nomadic life as a travel writer, and her bolt-hole to recharge throughout her career, it was also where she chose to retire, the perfect finale to an action-packed life.

The moment I'd stepped up to her door on that June day, I'd felt more at home than I expected. My nose twitched agreeably, full of the soft scent of May's apricot tea roses around the door. Slowly I swung it open, wondering whether I might find the house entirely empty. I hadn't thought to ask my dad, her executor, if the furniture was included.

To my relief, the fixtures and fittings were all still in place, as was the familiar smell of sandalwood and spice, exuded by the souvenirs she'd collected on her travels. Although I'd not been in the house for seven years (I felt dreadful when I did that sum), so much was still so familiar – the watercolour of Egyptian boats on the Nile just inside the door; the delicate Chinese plates hanging above the stairs; the Persian rugs in the little sitting room at the front of the house. I used to love visiting when I was younger, examining all her exotic souvenirs and hearing her tales of where she'd acquired them: jewel-bright Moroccan tea glasses; featherweight Japanese silk shawls; sinister Caribbean wood carvings. I envied her wild sense of fashion, culled eclectically from market stalls encountered on her travels.

It looked for all the world as if May still lived there.

Thirsty after my journey from Frankfurt, I set down my backpack and my suitcases in the hall and headed for the tiny kitchen-cum-dining-room. It's an old-fashioned kitchen with a stone sink, a wooden dresser, a few shelves, a couple of bentwood chairs and a small drop-leaf table pushed against one wall. In search of tea, I went through to the larder, a cool, dark room the size of a downstairs loo. I found a caddy of May's favourite Earl Grey, plus an unopened packet, alongside a pressed glass bowl of rainbow coffee sugar crystals. Even a cup of tea in Auntie May's house was an exotic experience. I'd forgotten how much I loved sprinkling those tiny jewels into the cup and watching them dissolve before adding a splash of milk from an almost translucent Japanese jug.

The sight of the new packet of teabags, that Auntie May had bought not knowing she'd never live to open it, was too much for me. I leaned back against the cool limestone wall and quietly wept.

After a little while, I wiped my face, feeling better. I acknowledged that this was the first of many times over the next few weeks that I would feel overwhelmed not just by bereavement, but by remorse for my neglect of Auntie May while she was still alive. I could never make up for lost time now.

I resolved to compensate in a different way: by making a real go of the opportunity she had given me to start afresh here and follow in her footsteps as a writer. Her writing genes would live on. I would be her phoenix.

Returning to the kitchen, I rinsed out the kettle, filled it with fresh water, brewed a china pot of Earl Grey, and took a tray loaded with pot, cup and saucer, spoon and sugar bowl into the back garden. I was thankful that someone had thoughtfully emptied the fridge and turned it off, so at least I hadn't inherited her last pint of milk. For once, I'd be happy to take my tea black.

As I stretched out gratefully on her rustic wooden bench, gnarled as an old man's knuckles, the sun went behind a cloud. I popped back inside for an extra layer and grabbed the silk shawl from the hallstand. Auntie May was the only person I have ever known who had an old-fashioned hallstand, which had been her mother's before her. Wrapping the shawl around my shoulders, I lay back on the bench to plan how I was going to make this work.

I had an awful lot of thinking to do.

Next thing I knew, I felt a bony hand touch my shoulder, and a scent as sharp as a freshly-opened bottle of bleach attacked my sinuses. When I opened my eyes, I half expected to find one of Damian's rural murderers looming over me with an axe. Instead, settling down in one of the garden armchairs opposite me was a tall, thin man with white hair and a handlebar moustache. I guessed him to be about eighty. The essence of mothballs emanated from his oatmeal tweed trousers and ginger corduroy waistcoat, worn over a checked flannel shirt. He was a real country boy if ever I saw one, and a bit old to be a murderer, or even a burglar. But I couldn't place why he looked familiar. Where had he come from? And what was he doing in my garden?

3

THE OLD BOY NEXT DOOR

The elderly gentleman watched me as I tried to get my bearings.

'Hello, my dear,' he said slowly, a twinkle in his pale blue eyes. 'Remember me? I'm May's boy next door. Joshua Hampton. Good day to you.'

I laughed, then hoped that hadn't sounded rude. 'Hello, I'm Sophie Sayers, May's great-niece,' I replied.

He raised his eyebrows.

'You didn't need to tell me that, my dear. You are the image of her. And in her favourite shawl, too.'

I drew the shawl tighter about me.

'I recognised you too,' I lied, though it was coming back to me now. I gathered there was some ancient feud, but I'd never got to the bottom of it. 'I'm sorry if my sudden appearance startled you. Did you know Auntie May had left her house to me in her will?'

Joshua sat back, sighing, and placed his hands, one on top of the other, on the handle of his walking stick.

'Yes, I did. In fact I knew about her will long before she passed away. I must say I approve. I'd far rather have her niece here than a bevy of strangers, piling in and changing things.'

He trailed off, gazing into the distance at the magnolia tree at the bottom of the garden. Now I looked at the garden properly, I recognised it was in sore need of some tidying up to restore it to Auntie May's high standard. She had kept it low-maintenance in her travelling days, but once she'd retired, developing it had been a substitute for foreign adventure. She brought the rest of the world to her tiny garden, importing interesting plants that had their origins far from home, challenging them to survive the Cotswold microclimate: Chinese acers, Greek fig trees, Japanese flowering cherries, Dutch bulbs in the spring. She even had a miniature version of Monet's pond, and often mentioned her garden's progress in the beautiful letters that she wrote to me every Friday while I was abroad, in the wonderfully evocative prose that had made her such a popular travel writer. Stupidly, I didn't keep her letters – too bent on travelling light. Nor did I have time to reply to them in kind, scribbling only a quick postcard whenever I ventured somewhere new. I thought she'd enjoy the feeling of travelling by proxy.

'Yes, it's still very much Auntie May's house. All her things are here. As you probably know, she didn't have any children who would have taken stuff away. My parents and I are her closest surviving relatives. My mum and dad live and work in Inverness, and I've been working abroad ever since I left university, so we've not really touched anything until now.'

'Yes, I know. I met your parents at May's funeral. They told me all about you.'

I blushed, guilty that I'd been unable to get leave from work to attend. Come to think of it, I was surprised Joshua had attended himself, unless it was to gloat. I wished I'd thought to ask May why they'd fallen out while I had the chance.

'How's your wife?' I asked, to make him aware that I knew something about him too.

'She passed away seven years ago, aged just seventy-six.'

'Oh, I'm sorry. How awful.'

'Thank you, my dear. But life goes on. I'm in my eighty-seventh year, you know. And there have been compensations.'

Perhaps he'd had his wife well insured. I could almost hear Damian's voice: well enough to make him hasten her demise?

'May's solicitor let me know that you'd be moving in this week,' he continued, 'so I've brought you a little housewarming present.'

From his trouser pocket, he produced a small glass jar full of a clear, dark liquid. At first I thought it an unhealthy urine sample, but it was too thick and slow-moving for that. I read the white sticky label written in a hand too shaky to be legible.

'Honey from my bees,' he prompted me. 'I hope you like honey. May used to stir a drop of my honey into her tea, to give her energy in the last months of her illness.'

That gave me a start. Had he been slowly poisoning Auntie May to seek a final victory in their feud? I held the jar up to the sunshine, which highlighted tiny flecks like minuscule insects in amber. Or were they grains of arsenic? Viewed through this prism, the sun took on an eerie, sickly glow. It didn't look like the life-giving superfood that honey is said to be.

I tried to remember exactly how honey is produced.

'Thank you. I'm sure I shall enjoy it.' Then I thought of a clever way to test my theory. 'Perhaps you'd like to come and have tea and scones with me one afternoon and we can eat it then?'

'I should like that very much.' Joshua leaned on his stick to raise himself to his feet. 'But I must leave you in peace to unpack, and wish you good evening. Next I shall go and tell my bees that you've arrived.' I must have looked at him oddly, because he went on to explain, 'You have to tell news to the bees, you know.'

I didn't know, but I wasn't about to admit it. He gave a little bow, and made his way down my back garden path. I wondered where he was going, until he turned right to depart via a gate through the wall to his own back garden. I didn't remember the gate being there last time I'd visited. Had he installed it after May's death to gain secret, easy access to her cottage? Now he could wander in and out of my property any time he liked, unseen by anyone but me. As indeed he just had.

Gazing thoughtfully at Joshua's honey, I turned to more immediate matters. I had nothing to spread it on. Apart from whatever Auntie May had left in her larder at the time of her death, there was no food in the house. I decided I'd better remedy that before the shops shut, or else my evening meal would have to consist of tea, sugar crystals, and stuff out of tins.

I knew there was a small grocery shop in the village, so I hauled myself up from the chair, returned my tea tray to the kitchen and locked the back door. Then I collected Auntie May's wicker shopping basket from its hook on the overhead airing rack, dropped my purse into it, and headed up the hill to the village shop. This dependable source of information might help me find out more about Joshua's reputation, and establish whether I could sleep safely in my bed that night while he was living next door.

4

THE ALPHABETICAL SHOP

The clouds of earlier in the afternoon had dispersed, and as I strolled up the High Street to the shop, I heard bees buzzing contentedly in the colourful front gardens. Auntie May had taught me the names of all the traditional cottagers' flowers: foxgloves, dahlias, marigolds, borage, scabious, everlasting wallflower. Lavender bushes bordered front paths like sentries, while less disciplined honeysuckle tumbled over fences and up tree trunks. May told me that knowing plant names would come in handy when I was older. Damian said it did, but only for crossword puzzles.

The front window of the shop was almost hidden by purple-flowered buddleias, a social club for butterflies now teeming with cabbage whites. Peering beyond the curtain of flowers into the small shop window, I noticed some changes since my last visit. It had clearly been given a makeover. Over the door, in sloping black hand-painted letters, the official statement of the shop's licence to sell alcohol informed me of a new proprietor: Carol Barker.

I slightly remembered Carol from my childhood visits. She

was a friend of my auntie May's, as were most of the villagers. Carol had cared for her bedridden mother in Pond Lane for many years, while her father ran the village shop. Muriel Barker had had a stroke but clung on for many years, unable to do much for herself other than prevent her daughter leading her own life. I guessed both mother and father must have died, leaving the family business to Carol, now aged about fifty.

I'd never seen much of Carol, other than when accompanying Auntie May to visit Muriel during my summer holidays. May always took as a gift a book, usually one of her own, 'so they can feel as if they're travelling without leaving their home'. It was generous of her, though I knew the books came from the small free stock the publisher gave her each time a new one was released.

Spending time with the Barkers must have made Auntie May appreciate her own freedom all the more. I'd felt stifled in their gloomy cottage, where the curtains were always closed and the windows tightly shut. I hoped running the shop had given Carol a new lease of life rather than an alternative prison.

As I pushed the door open, I recognised the distinctive jangling of the bell above my head. The shop's smell hadn't changed: a mixture of fresh bread, chilled cheese and newspapers, with the unmistakable whiff of furniture polish emanating from the old wooden shop counter.

'Why, if it isn't young Sophie Sayers!' cried Carol, springing up from the stool behind the till and laying down the copy of the *Daily Mail* she'd been reading. 'I heard you were moving to poor May's cottage. Goodness, look at you, if you aren't all grown up now!'

I shifted uncomfortably beneath her scrutiny. 'I am twenty-five, Carol, and it's my cottage now. May left it to me.'

She shrugged. 'It'll always be May Sayers's cottage to me, dear. When did you arrive?'

'Today, actually. So now I need to stock up my larder. Or at least get enough to tide me over till I can get to a supermarket.'

'Supermarkets are all very well, but make sure you use the village shop when you can, or the supermarket will be all you have. I keep telling people, if everyone in this village spent a fiver a week here, we'd do just fine. But do they, heck! I hope you'll do your best, anyway. I know it's what your auntie would have wanted.'

I bristled under this mild emotional blackmail, regretting my gaffe at mentioning the supermarket. There was no point in upsetting local people if I was going to make Wendlebury Barrow my new home.

'I want to get a few bits to start me off: bread, butter, eggs, cake, biscuits, chocolate and wine. Just the essentials.'

I turned around to look for those items. The shop is too small for shopping trolleys, so the convention is that you fill your own basket with whatever you need and empty it again at the counter before you pay. I made my way round the shop, noting the bright new decor. Carol had replaced the bottle green paintwork with refreshing shades of cream and pale blue, making the shop feel brighter, more spacious, at once retro and contemporary. She must have enjoyed being able to bask in bright light after being cooped up for so long with her invalid mother.

An array of home-made bread lay on the second shelf from the door, and I selected a white cottage loaf. Above the bread I spotted a packet of Bourbon biscuits, but what I really fancied was Scottish shortbread. When I asked Carol whether she had any, she pointed to the other side of the shop, where a small stack of tartan packets lay between a box of Sellotape and a mound of pink bathroom sponges.

When I couldn't find the eggs, she indicated a stack of grey cardboard cartons from the local free-range poultry farm. I remembered these as the best eggs I'd ever tasted, and probably the least travelled too. Next to the eggs lay a pile of *Daily Express* newspapers. Feeling a sudden need to connect with the British press after four years of living abroad, I asked whether she had any of the quality papers.

'You don't take the tablets?'

I was glad the conversation had turned to medicine, as it made it easier to enquire about May's last illness. Then I realised Carol meant the tabloids and shook my head.

'If it's *The Guardian* you want, you'll find it by the grapes, and *The Times* and *Telegraph* are over there next to the tomatoes and turnips. I can put by regular orders for you, if you like – daily papers or magazines. I get these two for Rex Hunter, for example.' She pulled out copies of *The Stage* and *Magic Week* from beneath the counter. 'Always happy to encourage our village drama club, of course. He's their director and I'm their wardrobe mistress, you know.' She made it sound as if they were an item. I was pleased for her.

Retracing my steps to the bread shelf to look for butter, I found none. When I asked Carol where it was, she smiled at me indulgently, shaking her head gently at my foolishness. 'In the chiller cabinet, of course. Between the apricot yoghurt and the cream.'

Of course. I soon filled my basket and returned to the counter for Carol to tot up my bill.

'Anything else I can help you with, dear? Are you settling in all right?'

I nodded. 'Yes, thank you. It is lovely to be here, though odd to think that it's not a holiday this time, and of course, I am so sad about Auntie May.'

She nodded, and for a moment I thought she was going to cry in sympathy, so I changed the subject. 'Joshua next door's already been round to welcome me. I was surprised, because I didn't think he and May got on. He never said a word to me when I used to come and stay with May in my school holidays.'

Almost dropping the eggs on the counter, Carol fixed me with a knowing look.

'Oh yes, they got on all right once his wife had died. He was good as gold to May after that, even collecting her prescriptions here when she got too frail to walk.'

I was shocked to hear that poor Auntie May had become too frail to take her daily march up to the shop. She'd always made me go with her, whether we needed something or not – she liked to support it, and insisted on a daily constitutional to blow away the cobwebs. I'd had to almost run to keep up with her.

I'd forgotten the shop also acted as an intermediary between the doctor's surgery and the pharmacy. I could see on the shelf behind Carol a neat row of dispensed prescriptions, all bagged up and discreetly labelled, so no-one could see the contents. But if I'd a mind to, I could have reached out and taken one off the shelf. I could even have swapped the contents with someone else's while Carol's back was turned. As could Joshua.

On the counter lay a small clipboard of repeat prescription requests. On top was a note from one Linda Absolom – I might have guessed they would be in alphabetical order. Beside the clipboard was a well-thumbed thick paperback.

'That's the formulary,' Carol said, seeing me looking at it. She sounded proud. 'It's what doctors and pharmacists use to look up medicines, to check doses and side-effects. I use it to make sure people have spelled things right when they write a request for a repeat prescription. And if anyone asks what their medicine is for, I can look it up and tell them. All part of the service. It keeps people coming back to the shop. Minnie Jenkins was very impressed when I said her pink ointment was for haemorrhoids. She thought she just had piles.'

I assumed it was standard practice for people to pick each other's items up. 'I suppose Joshua had got in the habit of collecting prescriptions for his late wife too?'

'Ooh no, her end came right out of the blue. Edith just dropped dead all of a sudden one day. Heart failure, it was, with no real warning. Except of course I knew she'd been on heart tablets for a while. Beetle-blockers, she had.'

Damian's comments leapt into my head again. Had Joshua bumped off Edith with a bit of his honey one tea-time, drugged with something to stop her heart? Then I thought of Joshua's kind eyes, his old-fashioned manners and his charm. Psychopaths could fake charm, but something didn't quite click.

I determined to exorcise myself of Damian's influence.

'Anything else I can get you?' Carol brought me back into the moment. 'Like to place any regular orders for bread, milk, papers, parish mag? Regular orders are the lifeblood of the village shop. Use it or lose it.'

To keep in with her, I signed up for all of those things, though wasn't sure that the parish magazine would provide exciting reading. Then turning to go, I noticed the board by the shop door displaying advertisements on postcards. I glanced over them to see whether they offered anything I might need. Although I had no use for outgrown children's bicycles or baby rabbits or surplus topsoil, this would be the perfect place to advertise my services as an ELT teacher, to generate a bit of income before I began to earn serious money as an author. I'd need some form of wage to afford to stay here in the meantime, even though I could live rent free.

'How much do you charge to display a postcard, please, Carol?' I asked.

'Ooh, no charge, dear, the board's just there as a service to villagers. You'll find the postcards between the plums and the potatoes. What are you wanting to advertise?'

As I started to tell her, the shop bell jangled and an old boy entered, wearing wellingtons and ancient twill trousers with braces over his string vest.

'I teach English as a foreign language.'

He gave a hearty laugh.

'English as a foreign language? You won't find any foreigners round these parts, girlie. Saving yourself, of course. And that poncey Mr and Mrs Absolom who just moved into Jay Cottage. They came from up that London five years ago. I can't understand what they're saying with their la-di-dah ways. You might try giving them a lesson or two.'

'Oh, Billy, now don't you be so rude to young Sophie, she's doing her best,' said Carol. 'She's only trying to keep the fox from the door, and that's to be encouraged. You won't find May Sayers's niece putting her feet up and living off state pension and benefits, unlike some I could name.'

Her pointed jibe washed over Billy who went to search through the alphabet for a can of stout.

'But I'm afraid he's right, my dear, we don't have anyone living in the village who isn't a native English speaker. You'd have to drive into Gloucester to find anyone like that, though I dare say you'd find plenty when you got there. If it's a job in the village that you're looking for, I suggest you try Hector's House. I hear he's got a vacancy.'

'He's a bit vacant, more like,' called Billy from by the S shelf. 'That man wants to spend more time with the real world and less with his books.'

'Hector's house? Thanks, Carol, but it's not a cleaning job I'm after. I need something a bit more cerebral.'

'Cerebral? What, like Weetabix?' Billy, pausing by some cans of Whitbread, helpfully waved a yellow packet from the W–Z section.

'Not cereal, Billy, cerebral,' I called to him. 'That means brainy.'

'Not your special subject, Billy.'

Carol waved her hand in his direction dismissively. Billy put down the Weetabix, picked up a four-pack of stout and flipped open one of the ring-pulls as he came to queue behind me.

Carol got the conversation back on track quickly. 'I don't mean Hector's house, I mean Hector's *House*. Remember the old antique shop up the High Street? Belonged to old Mr and Mrs Munro? Well, they moved to the seaside a few years ago, and gave the shop lease over to their son, Hector. He's turned it into a nice, clean bookshop, much better than those dusty old antiques. Successful, too, by all accounts. He's even got a little tea shop in there, and he's so supportive of other villagers.'

'Tea shop, my arse!' muttered Billy. 'We all know about Hector's tea.'

'Ssssh!' said Carol quickly. 'It's a tea shop, and no mistake. And his buns are so fancy, Sophie, you wouldn't believe them unless you saw them.'

'And as to his buns...'

I thought it best to cut Billy's conversation short, said goodbye and left. However, I determined to head to Hector's House the next day, once I'd finished unpacking. I was sure Auntie May would have approved. She'd encouraged me to write, giving me beautiful notebooks, exquisitely tooled pens and padlocked diaries that she'd brought back from exotic locations on her travels. I think she'd regarded me as the daughter she never had, hoping I'd continue her line after she'd gone.

I hoped Hector stocked May's books in his bookshop. But I was even more eager to discover the secret of Hector's special tea. Not another local source of poison, surely?

5

CLEAN SHEETS

Before I dared try my luck at Hector's House, I thought I'd better get myself organised. After travelling from Frankfurt early that morning, following a sleepless night worrying about missing the plane, I had neither my wits nor my CV about me. If I was serious about trying for a job, I wanted to give it my best shot. This meant showering, changing, and revising my employment history to make it look as if all my life so far had been building up to working in a bookshop.

It wasn't hard to feel enthusiastic – I was looking forward to starting afresh and reinventing myself. No longer would I be a bored peripatetic teacher in a failing relationship. Now that I had my own permanent home – or a home as permanent as I chose to make it – I hoped the work would somehow fall into place. A relationship could come later. In my experience, relationships don't pay the bills. Quite the opposite, in fact.

I wondered what this Hector would be like. His name made him sound old and grumpy, and I hoped he wouldn't be the sort of boss who would make my life a misery. I decided to prepare as thoroughly as I could before approaching him.

Taking a much-needed ham sandwich and a cup of tea into the sitting room, I sank down onto the green Chesterfield, wondering how on earth May had managed to get such a chunky piece of furniture in through the narrow front door of the cottage. As I gazed around, chewing, I spotted on the bookshelf beneath the window the old wooden flower press Auntie May and I used to preserve whatever flowers took my fancy in her garden or on our strolls around the surrounding lanes. Together we'd painstakingly lay them out, uncurling every petal on the blotting paper sheets. Then we'd stack them on top of each other like the layers of *mille-feuille* pastry, before replacing the plywood square on top and screwing down the nuts on the bolts at the corners as far as we dared. At the beginning of my next visit, we'd release the pressed flowers from where they'd lain all year, before gluing them down onto cards for framing or turning them into bookmarks for my parents. The dried versions were only ever pale echoes of the original flowers. But more importantly, they preserved the quality time we'd spent together.

After finishing my sandwich, I washed up the plate and mug then headed upstairs with my rucksack to unpack. At first I turned into the tiny guest bedroom in the attic where I'd slept during my childhood visits. It was even smaller than I remembered. The only furniture was an ancient brass bed, spread with its familiar patchwork quilt in faded yellow floral prints, and a small chest of drawers. This was enough for what I'd brought for my fortnight's summer holiday, but not for a grown-up's permanent bedroom.

I felt my heart flutter as I crossed the small landing to Auntie May's room. I would not have been surprised to find her sitting up in bed drinking tea.

Like the guest room, it was almost unchanged from when I'd last seen it. Her favourite face cream and perfume stood on the pine dressing table, but lying in one of the scarlet Venetian glass trinket dishes was a purple and white rubber band bracelet, which could only have been made the previous summer, when every other child in the developed world was busy making jewellery out of those tiny rings. I wondered who had made it for her, feeling a foolish pang of jealousy that there had been another child in her life besides me.

I half fell onto the stool in front of the dressing table, steeling myself to claim May's bedroom, and her bed, as my own. Despite the warm evening, I shivered as I wondered whether she had died sleeping in the sheets that were on the bed. Then I leapt up and turned back the eiderdown for evidence.

To my relief, beneath the eiderdown was the bare mattress. I was grateful to the anonymous housekeeper for not disturbing May's personal effects elsewhere in the room.

On the nightstand lay her small folding alarm clock with the luminous green figures, which I knew to have been her constant companion in her travelling days. Beside the clock was propped a small Moleskine notebook with a dark green cover. She always had one of these on the go, and she had three shelves full of them downstairs in the alcove above her writing desk, the raw material of her many published travelogues. The stump of a pencil lay beside this one, worn down to its last few inches. I wondered whether she knew, when she bought the pencil, that it would outlive her. Without thinking, I plucked a few tissues from the squat cardboard box behind the alarm clock. I'd dried my eyes and blown my nose before it occurred to me that she must have touched the one on top as she lay dying.

Then I remembered that I didn't even know whether she had died at home or in hospital. Another wave of guilt washed over me at the thought that as she was breathing her last, I was hundreds of miles away, preoccupied with something as unimportant as coaching German children to conjugate English verbs.

A knock at the back door made me pull myself together. Scrubbing quickly at my cheeks with another tissue, I ran down the stairs, forgetting the low beam halfway down and banging my head. When I flung open the back door, I saw two of Joshua standing on the path, and wondered for a moment whether he was one of twins.

As the two Joshuas merged into one, I noticed that in his arms lay a pile of fresh bedlinen.

'You'll need these tonight,' he said, ignoring my discomposure. 'May's sheets. I thought you'd appreciate fresh laundry on the bed when you arrived.'

I took them and backed into the kitchen, beckoning him in for the sake of politeness, but feeling slightly uncomfortable, not to mention mildly concussed. Damian would have accused him of sneaking the linen from May's deathbed to wash out the evidence of wrong-doing.

'Did... did you wash them, or did someone else do that after she died?' I asked, fumbling for the right words. It struck me that he could easily have murdered May in her bed, especially if she was weakened by her illness. 'I mean, I wasn't sure whether she died in hospital, or—'

I ground to a halt, staring at the floor till he put me out of my misery.

'May was in a hospice for the last few days. She knew she wouldn't be coming back. She asked me to make the house ready for you when you came. I was glad to be able to do something useful for her when otherwise I felt so helpless.'

Looking up, I saw his grey eyes fill with tears. Not another actor in my life, I thought resentfully. They are always so dramatic. But while he was here, I might as well take advantage of his local knowledge.

I set the clean sheets down on the kitchen table and pulled out one of the chairs.

'Here, stop and have a cup of tea with me, Joshua. I was about to make one. And then I'd like to ask your advice about something.'

He smiled. 'Of course.'

As he sat down, I filled the kettle and began to tell him my dilemma.

'You see, I'm treating this whole inheritance thing as an opportunity to make a career change, in a direction that I know Auntie May would have wanted. I'm going to be a writer, like her, though not necessarily writing about travel. A peaceful, sleepy village like this would be the perfect place for me to start, and where better than at Auntie May's old desk, surrounded by her books? But while I'm writing the first one and getting it published – getting on the authorial ladder, so to speak – I'll need to earn my keep some other way. I was hoping I could find local pupils who need some English as a Foreign Language lessons.'

Joshua let out a staccato laugh. I didn't need him to tell me he shared Billy's assessment of the local market for EFL lessons.

'But plan B is to get a job at the village bookshop. I didn't even know there was a village bookshop till Carol told me just now. It was still an antique shop last time I came to visit May.'

Joshua looked reproachful. 'It's about five years since Gordon and Shona Munro retired and their son turned it into a bookshop.'

I nodded, embarrassed by the reminder of my long absence. 'The thing is, that would be a really fitting place for a writer to earn a bit of bread-and-butter money. Carol in the shop told me that the proprietor is looking for an assistant, so I'm steeling myself to go and apply tomorrow. What do you think? Do you know this man? Any clues as to how I should approach him?'

Joshua chuckled.

'Young Hector Munro? I've known him since he was a nipper, though he went away to university and didn't come back for a long time, except for occasional family visits. That's why you never met him. A man of singular habits, he's done a lot of good for this village: brought in visitors with his fancy antics, provided a pleasant venue for us locals to go and enjoy a cup of tea together. Not in competition with the pub, mind you – he's careful not to take any business from the pub, nor the village shop. Yes, there's plenty of room in this village for the likes of Hector Munro.'

'So is it a fancy bookshop? More Hatchards than W H Smith?'

I was warming to the idea. A posh bookshop would be a much better source of inspiration than one that earned its keep selling trashy romances. Though I couldn't see how a bookshop could possibly compete with a pub.

Joshua leaned forward and rapped on the kitchen table with his knuckles. 'Do you know, I don't think there's any other bookshop in the country quite like Hector's House. You could do a lot worse than get in with Hector, my dear. It would be a fine way to make new friends in the village too, and to get yourself known as something other than May's long-lost niece.'

'I was never exactly lost.'

I was saved from digging myself into a bigger hole by the sound of the kettle boiling.

Returning to the table with a cup of tea in each hand, I diverted the conversation on to less self-damning territory.

'I'm surprised that a bookshop can remain in business in such a remote spot. There must be a lot of keen readers in the village, and no library nearby to borrow books from.'

'Oh, there's a library all right, down the road a few miles in Slate Green, but it's not the same experience as a visit to Hector's House. He's a smart man who has learned a lot from the few farmers still in business around here. Diversifying, that's his secret.'

'What, you mean like offering bed and breakfast?'

'Not exactly, though there was a rumour that old Billy once accidentally got locked in the shop overnight after a particularly convivial meeting of the Village Show Committee in the tearoom. Let's say Hector's got plenty of other ideas to keep his business ticking over comfortably, including a few cards he plays close to his chest. He's a bit of a man of mystery, is our Hector. If your application is successful, you may find out some of his secrets. Or maybe you won't.'

I was beginning to wonder whether applying for a job as his assistant was such a good idea. What if Hector turned out to be a contract killer, having inherited the position as head of the local village mafia from his father? Or godfather?

'If you need a referee, do not hesitate to give my name. Although if you tell him you're May's niece, you'll be in. He owes her a few favours. She used to bring so many customers in there for her book launches in the last few years. His shop was always her first port of call when she had a new book out, even before the big literary festivals or the Cheltenham bookshops. She was loyal to her village, was May, no matter how far away she ventured on her travels. Loyal to her village.'

His voice petered out, and he gazed into the distance. I tried to bring him back to the present.

'What do you think I should wear for the interview?' Only after I'd spoken did I realise I should not be asking fashion advice from a man in his eighties who, I'd just noticed, was wearing mismatched shoes. I guessed his eyesight must be failing. To be fair, as a tall man, his head was a long way from his feet.

'Something officey or artistic? What's more Hector's style?'

'Hector's style? Hector's a one-off. I reckon he'd prefer something unconventional. Idiosyncratic. Expressive. Certainly not an office suit. Wear what makes you feel comfortable, my dear, and what you'd like to see a lady in a bookshop wearing.'

I tried to think of the last time I'd really looked at the clothes of the person serving me in a bookshop, or even been in a proper bookshop. I thought I'd probably always been looking at the book rather than the bookseller.

'And something that isn't too hot. It's going to be a scorcher tomorrow, looking at that sky tonight.'

He pointed an arthritic finger towards the kitchen window, where a still-bright sun lit up the apple blossom.

'Perhaps I should raid Auntie May's wardrobe for something arty looking.'

'Blue stockings, you mean? You could do a lot worse.' Joshua drained his teacup and raised himself unsteadily to his feet.

As he reached the back door, he turned to look at me again, and ran a slow appraising eye over me from head to toe that set me a-shiver.

He closed the door gently behind him, and pottered down the path to the gate between May's garden and his – I mean, *my* garden and his. I hoped I wasn't going to follow in her footsteps in every respect and end up murdered in my bed, poisoned by a dose of Joshua's honey administered by one of Hector's contract killers.

I'd better make sure my interview went well.

6

HECTOR'S HOUSE

'Hello, can you tell me where Hector is, please? Carol in the village shop told me that he needs help.'

'You can say that again,' came a familiar voice from the back corner. Arranged around three circular tin tables were a dozen old-fashioned folding garden chairs, one of them occupied by Billy, the non-cerebral stout-drinker from the day before. Despite the aspersions he'd cast on Hector's tea, he was enthusiastically working his way through a large pot of the stuff.

A lean olive-skinned man in his early thirties was leaning on the main shop counter with his arms folded, longish dark curls flopping forward to cover his high forehead.

'I can. But should I?'

Confused, I glanced across at Billy for a clue. That was a mistake.

'She'll be asking to see your buns next, Hector.'

'Thank you, Billy, if I need your advice, I'll ask for it.'

The man at the counter unfolded his arms and pointed one finger at his chest. 'He's here. I'm Hector. Thank you for brightening my bookshop with your presence. I don't believe we've met before?'

Despite Hector's parents having only recently retired, I'd been picturing someone only marginally less aged than himself. After all, when you're eighty-six, most people qualify as younger. Perhaps it was the archaic name that threw me. Hectors should be wrinkly grey-haired curmudgeons in cardigans, not gorgeous, enigmatic Greek gods.

Hector held out a warm, soft hand for me to shake, before coming out from behind the counter to stand alongside me. 'But the more pressing question for me is, how can I help you? No, don't tell me, I've got just the book for you.'

He strode over to the fiction section, plucked a paperback from among the Gs and presented it to me, deadpan.

'Here we are: *Travels with my Aunt* by Graham Greene.'

Billy guffawed. 'Point to you, young Hector!'

I gasped. 'How did you know who I was? Did you recognise her skirt?'

I'd put on a long mulberry velvet one from my aunt's wardrobe to try to look cultured.

'Have you looked in the mirror lately?' replied Hector. 'You are obviously related to May Sayers. Billy tells me that you're living in May's cottage.'

'Actually, my name's on the deeds now. My great aunt left the cottage to me.'

'You'll have to wait about twenty years before people round here call it your cottage. Your name being...?'

'Sophie. Sophie Sayers. Sayers, same as my aunt.'

'Yes, you certainly are,' put in Billy, who clearly considered himself part of our conversation. 'Don't let old Joshua see you looking like that, whatever you do. It'll be too much for him. We'll be carrying him off to the graveyard to lie alongside her, if you're not careful.'

Hector shot him a withering look. 'Billy, really! Drink your tea or I'll take it away.'

That shut him up. He must have needed the tea to sober him up after his early start on the stout the previous afternoon.

In the ensuing silence, I noticed for the first time the music that was playing softly in the background: Mike Oldfield's *Tubular Bells*. Great Auntie May had long ago taught me to love this classic album from the 70s. It's not something you hear much in public these days.

'You're playing—'

Hector's smile had a hint of smugness about it. 'Your tune? Your Auntie May always loved it, so I thought you might too.'

'What? Did you see me coming and put it on specially?'

'Spot on.'

We both listened appreciatively for a moment to the music's gentle meanderings, while he set the Graham Greene book on the counter, facing me, presumably as a hint. But I wasn't so easily hoodwinked by his charm into buying a book I neither wanted nor needed. May's house was stuffed with books.

I pulled myself together, remembering the serious and pressing intent of my visit. If I wasn't able to get a job here, I'd have to look further afield, and soon.

'So, as I was saying, Carol Barker said you were looking for an assistant. And Joshua Hampton, next door to me, encouraged me to apply. So please may I have an application form?'

Hector patted his pockets as if searching. 'Sorry, I seem to be fresh out of them. Bit of a run on applications this morning. How about an application cup of tea instead?'

He gestured to the tearoom. I chose the table furthest from Billy.

'So, tea?' offered Hector, sitting down opposite me. 'Not you, Billy, you've had enough for one morning.'

Behind me, Billy drained his cup noisily, and scraped his chair across the old oak floorboards. 'No matter, I'll be heading off to The Bluebird for my dinner soon.'

'But it's only eleven o'clock.' I wondered what scenic route he'd be taking to the village pub, a few hundred yards away, to make his journey last till evening.

'That's The Bluebird's opening time. I has a ploughman's lunch up there for my dinner midday every Tuesday. Washed down with a nice pint of old Donald's special. Good luck with your interview, girlie.'

He rolled the word interview around his mouth like a euphemism for some lascivious delight.

The shop door jangled to allow Billy's exit as Hector set down a loaded tea tray on the table between us. The crockery was decorated with the titles of classic novels in old-fashioned typewriter fonts. He'd given me Charles Dickens's *Great Expectations* and himself Somerset Maugham's *Cakes and Ale*. The teapot was branded *Love in a Cold Climate* by Nancy Mitford.

'Nice china,' I couldn't help but remark.

'Yes, it is, isn't it? I get it free from the Literally Gifted mail order company, in return for plugging their website on my shop's bookmarks. It's an arrangement that suits all parties. I don't see the point in paying for something when I can get someone else to provide it for free. I make a good margin on their stock that I sell here too.' He indicated a dresser displaying fancy stationery and houseware with bookish themes. 'I'm always on the lookout for opportunities to make a bit of money in other ways than selling books. Otherwise I wouldn't have a bookshop at all.'

He settled down again opposite me and sat back in the chair, which creaked slightly, though there wasn't a gramme of spare fat on him. 'So, why would you like to work in my bookshop? Why should I employ you rather than any of the many other applicants? What would you bring to the game that others can't?'

I took a deep breath; I'd been anticipating this question. While awaiting my answer, he poured us each some tea.

'I'm a local resident so I'd always be on time for work, being within easy walking distance. Plus, you'd have the satisfaction of knowing you were creating local employment for a fellow villager.' I'd taken on board what Joshua had said about Hector being supportive to the community. 'And, as a writer myself, I have a great interest in books.'

'Oh, really? Have you written anything I might have heard of? Anything stocked on my shelves?'

He swept his arm around to indicate his small empire, inviting me to point out my title.

'I haven't exactly had any books published yet, not to speak of.'

'Oh, you're self-published? That's fine by me, provided your books will fly off the shelves and make me a decent profit. Readers don't care who's published a book as long as it's a good read.'

I grimaced, wondering how to break it to him that I wasn't published in any shape or form. I bought time to think by taking a few sips of tea. It was surprisingly astringent, but in a bracing kind of way. I assumed he hadn't rinsed the washing-up liquid off the china.

'I haven't self-published any books, either, though that's probably the route I'll be taking.'

He nodded sagely. 'Good, I like a girl with ambition. Are you good at dealing with customers?'

'Oh, I'm very good with people. I've spent the last four years abroad, teaching children and adults to speak English. That takes a lot of patience and tact. And I'm good at making sense of what people say, even if they're not using the right words. I'm sure that must come in handy in a bookshop.'

Hector got up to fetch me a small chocolate cupcake from the tearoom counter. On top of the pale violet icing lay a white chocolate letter S, sprinkled with hundreds and thousands.

'Gosh, that looks lovely.'

'Yes, I'm famous for my buns.' Deadpan again. I couldn't judge whether he was laughing at me, whether this was meant to be a practical diplomacy test, or simply indicated that he was happy to continue the interview for long enough for me to eat a cake.

'I don't make them myself,' he added. 'I buy them in from a lady in the village, Mrs Wetherley, and I pay her in books. She makes them specially for me.'

I'd remembered that Joshua had tipped me off about Hector diversifying for the sake of profitability. Here was an opportunity asking to be seized.

'Surely you ought to be selling more than that? You could make them up into little boxes, and offer whole words for sale, like you see in sweetshops, with tiny lettered bars of chocolate to make up into names. Your lady ought to be more business-like. If you packaged them in boxes with a smart business name on the side, they'd be brilliant gifts. And she could do bigger ones, to order, as birthday cakes. Or rectangular cakes, decorated to look like books, with appropriate titles iced on top. You could brand them 'The Birthday Letters' like the Ted Hughes book. I reckon they'd fly out the door.' Emboldened by his broadening smile, I continued. 'Or how about 'Eat My Words'? Oh no, hang on, that sounds like the tell-all confession of a corrupt encyclopaedia salesman!'

'Ha! Encyclopaedias! Now there's a concept from the past. It's all Google and Wikipedia these days. You may be young, but I suspect you're an old-fashioned girl at heart, Sophie Sayers.'

He pulled a pen and a pad of Post-it notes from his trouser pocket and scribbled something down – the first notes he'd made during our entire interview. I took this to be a promising sign.

'I guess I am, or I wouldn't be applying for a job in a village bookshop!' To my surprise, I was beginning to feel curiously relaxed, comfortable enough now to tease him back a little.

'And you seem full of bright ideas. God knows, we need bright ideas to keep this shop open. Any form of diversification that'll help keep us afloat. Do you think you can come up with new ideas to put us back into profit?'

I nodded, even though my head at that point felt entirely empty of inspiration. Then I thought of an intelligent remark.

'Don't you ever worry, Hector, that people might spill coffee on books before they buy them? I mean, the tearoom is awfully close to the shelves.'

'Not really.'

He pointed to a small handwritten sign above the coffee machine, which said, 'Penalty for spilling coffee on books: twice the cover price, once for the cost of the book and once to teach you to treat books with more respect.'

'So at least if it happens, I sell a book. Okay, one last question, then.'

I took a longer swig of tea to fortify me. This sounded like a make-or-break question.

'Are you any good with a Nespresso machine?' Hector indicated a shiny red one beside the cake stands.

'I sure am. What writer doesn't like a cup of coffee?' I was starting to believe my own PR, always a dangerous sign.

'Then you're hired. Five days a week, plus every other Saturday, so I can push off on alternative weekends. We don't open on

Sundays. I'm putting you in charge of the tearoom, by the way, and any tips are all yours.'

I opened my mouth to gasp in astonishment. When I hiccupped instead, I felt less embarrassed than I should have done.

'Don't you want any references first? My CV?'

'Nah. May Sayers and Joshua Hampton are good enough for me. And if you're anything like your old auntie, we'll get on like a house on fire.'

He pushed back his chair, stood up and stretched. Then he sat down again, all of a sudden. Elbows on the table, he leaned forward and looked into my eyes. I tried to concentrate on how green they were to calm my nerves.

'I'll level with you,' he said in a low voice. 'Employing a second member of staff is essential if I'm to be able to keep the shop open nine till five, six days a week, instead of closing up whenever I need to go off and do something else. You are potentially the saviour of Hector's House. Or not.'

I forced a smile. 'No pressure then.'

The news alarmed me slightly – I'd hate my first impression in the village to be as the girl who put the local bookshop out of business. But it also flooded me with a sense of importance. At least here was a job in which I would really feel that I was making a difference – valued not as one in a series of itinerant teachers who would be called by the name of my predecessor for at least the first term in a new school, but as an individual. I could be someone. I could be a contender.

I smiled and held out my hand for him to shake. His handshake was firm, but gentle; confident, but not crushing.

'Deal. And by the way, there weren't any other candidates. You were the only one. But don't let that prevent you from celebrating your success.'

I laughed. 'Funnily enough, I'm feeling in quite a party mood now.'

He tapped the teapot. 'That'll be the tea. Didn't you notice?'

When he lifted the lid, I leaned over it and sniffed, catching for the first time the unmistakable whiff of alcoholic spirits.

'Oh my God, what on earth is that?' I clutched my throat. 'Help, I've been poisoned!'

He laughed, unperturbed. 'Just another little way to lure customers into the shop and keep them happy. Now, I suggest you start tomorrow, bright and early at 9 a.m., which is when we open on weekdays, ready for our first rush of tearoom business after the mums have dropped their kids off at the village school.'

We got up and headed back towards the shop counter.

'Oh, and take this on the house as your starter for ten.' He thrust the copy of *Travels with my Aunt* into my hand, and wrapped around it a dog-eared copy of *The Bookseller* magazine. 'Because you'll never get time to read while you're working here.'

After thanking him profusely, I left the store as a bookseller. I wondered how many people I was about to lead astray in the remarkable Hector's House tearoom, and whether all of them would walk out the door relatively unscathed, like me. Or could Hector's House be the book trade's equivalent of Sweeney Todd's?

I resolved to stick to his coffee in future.

7

MONEY IN BOOKS

'Carol, I cannot thank you enough!'

Entering the village shop, I threw the door against the wall, setting the bell jangling as if possessed.

'Been drinking Hector's tea this morning, have you?' Carol smiled knowingly.

'I start work there tomorrow as a bookseller.' I hiccupped. 'And it's you I have to thank for that.'

Carol brushed my thanks aside with a wave of her hand. 'Least I can do for you, my dear, after all your Auntie May's kindness to me and my late mother, though she must have known I could never repay her.'

I put my hand over my mouth to disguise another hiccup. 'Actually, Joshua Hampton encouraged me too, and offered to give me a reference. But I didn't need one. The interview was enough to swing it. It was a very good interview.'

I stepped over to the counter and rested my book and magazine on it, before leaning forward to whisper confidentially, 'Hector is awfully handsome, don't you think?'

Carol took a step backwards. 'So some say. A bit hard to pin down, though, by all accounts.'

'You mean he's single?'

She nodded. 'Don't go getting any ideas there, Sophie. I've got him down as a confirmed bachelor, if you know what I mean.'

It took me a moment to catch her drift. 'Oh, I see. That's a pity. Still, he is lovely, don't you think? And he has given me a job. So now I'm in the mood to celebrate. I thought I'd buy some scones to share with Joshua.' I put on an innocent voice, hoping it might winkle out any secrets about him. 'He brought me some of his honey yesterday. Wasn't that kind?'

'You are privileged,' said Carol. 'Several ladies in the village have tried to get their hands on his honey and failed. That rude new woman round the corner, Mrs Absolom, is always pestering me to stock it in the shop. I don't know why she can't just go and ask him for some herself. It's not as if she's usually backward in coming forward.' She tapped the side of her nose meaningfully. 'I reckon she's been having a bit of a fling with that Rex. Though to be fair, her husband's just as bad, running off with that woman from his office. Six of one and a dozen of the other, if you ask me.'

That made me reconsider my assessment of Carol and Rex. If they had been an item, they clearly weren't any more.

'So you reckon his honey's all right then?'

Carol nodded. 'I don't see why not.'

With aluminium tongs, she lifted four scones from a plastic tray on the counter, and popped them into a paper bag. 'That'll be £1.20 please, love.'

As I fished the exact change out of my skirt pocket, she dropped the tongs on the floor, dusted them off on her apron and set them back among the cakes and pastries. Hugging the paper bag close to my chest, I all but skipped out of the shop and back to May's cottage. I went straight out of the back door and let myself through the gate to Joshua's garden, where he stood weeding a raised bed of tomatoes. Hector's tea had made me feel less nervous of him.

'Guess what?'

'You got the job?'

I beamed, and held out the bag of scones. 'Come on, let's celebrate! Honey and scones all round.'

He followed me into my garden, and I went inside to bring out a tea tray laden with honey, butter and May's tea things. I set them down on the table in front of the bench by the garden window. Joshua was studying me carefully as I stumbled.

'Have you been celebrating already?'

'Yes, I confess, I did have some of Hector's tea. But I think the effects are wearing off now, and the scones will absorb the rest of the alcohol. Honestly, I wonder how he gets away with it.'

'Lack of customer complaints?' suggested Joshua, turning his rheumy eyes to my long skirt. I was glad I wasn't wearing a short one. 'My goodness, you are indeed the echo of your aunt.'

'*Great* aunt,' I reminded him.

'Great indeed,' he replied, then coughed and changed the subject. 'So, how are you settling in?'

I poured us each a cup of tea, considering the best reply. 'Last night it felt odd sleeping in her bed, instead of the guest bed. It will take me a while to think of her bed as my bed. I thought sitting at her writing desk to put together my CV would inspire me, but I just felt inadequate, thinking of how many bestselling books she's written there. Maybe I need to set up my own writing space somewhere different, like a writing hut in the garden. Roald Dahl had a lovely garden shed to write in. I've seen it in his museum, in Great Missenden. He used to write surrounded by all his favourite things.'

I stared down the garden to consider where I might put a

shed. 'But what am I thinking? I've already got the very thing.' I pointed to the small stone outhouse at the end of the garden. I'd never been allowed to play in it when staying with May as a child. 'What a perfect writing den that would make! Who could fail to be inspired down there? I wonder why Auntie May never used it herself.'

Joshua gave me what Auntie May would have called an old-fashioned look. 'Oh, but I think she did, in her younger days, but not for the purposes you have in mind.'

I wondered what on earth she'd got up to in there.

'Go on, go and take a look. There are no monsters in there, I assure you. Perhaps it's not what you're expecting, but it's provided the perfect spot for quiet thought for generations.'

Unsure of his meaning, I ventured down the garden path. Before opening the door, I looked back at him for reassurance, and he nodded encouragement. I lifted the ancient rusting latch and pulled hard on the handle. It swung back all of a sudden to reveal the outhouse's unmistakable purpose. Before me was a broad horizontal wooden plank from wall to wall, with a large oval-shaped hole in the centre. Beneath the hole stood an old-fashioned enamel bucket. Halfway up the stone wall, hanging from a nail, was a handful of newspaper squares strung together. I bent closer to examine them. They were dated 1947.

Joshua called out to me down the garden path. 'It was a great day when they brought mains plumbing to the village after the war.'

Gently I pushed the door to and lifted the latch to close it securely.

'I'll think on it,' I conceded, retracing my steps back to Joshua.

'You won't be the first. But stick to following in your great aunt's footsteps, my dear, and all will come right in the end.'

I nodded. 'Auntie May thought so too, even though the careers advisor at school told me that writing could never be a viable career. That's why I took up teaching instead. Even so, Auntie May always used to tell me there was money in books. I think she thought I'd get round to it eventually. She approved of my travelling to find subject matter to write about, even if it wasn't the adventurous kind of travel that she did.'

Before tucking into a scone, Joshua stared at me for a moment. I had the feeling there was something he wanted to tell me. I thought I'd better not press him, in case it was something I didn't want to hear. Instead, I poured us each a second cup of tea.

Only when I was clearing away the tea things after he'd gone did I realise that neither of us had touched the honey.

8

BACK TO THE WRITING DESK

Although I wasn't sure yet what I should write, that evening I sat down at Auntie May's old-fashioned wooden bureau. I pulled down the flap to expose the maze of pigeonholes that used to fascinate me as a child. Each was filled with a different kind of stationery, the essentials of her craft: lined paper for handwritten drafts; plain paper for sketches; her latest diaries and notebooks that provided the raw material for her next book; pencils, pens, erasers, rulers, staples, treasury tags. All neatly stored in little boxes within the many nooks.

On the shelf above was a dusty old travelling typewriter. This had been her workhorse in the early years of her writing life, though latterly it had been more of an ornament. Her modern laptop was concealed in a drawer below, and her printer was on the floor. I couldn't bring myself to log in to her laptop yet, though it crossed my mind there might be some unfinished manuscript lurking there that I should send to her publisher.

Like May, I'd travelled extensively, but I was more of a tourist. I may have become familiar with the local museums, parks, galleries and restaurants, but I never really went native. Would

anyone else want to read an account of my experience in each
city? A shudder ran through me. No, the only travel book I was
qualified to write was a cautionary tale on how to be a tourist
instead of a traveller.

One summer, when I was about fifteen and staying with May,
a sumptuous glossy brochure had arrived in the post, offering her
and a companion of her choice a free trip on the latest upmarket
cruise ship in return for her writing about it. By the time I'd
pored over the alluring pictures of the glamorous life on board, I
was longing for her to ask me to be Passepartout to her Phileas
Fogg. I'd nickname her Philomena Fogg on the journey, and I
hoped I could persuade her to take a carpet bag.

I'd been horrified when she turned down the offer without
even reading the brochure.

'It's not for nothing that my monthly column in the *Traveller*
magazine is called 'Under My Own Steam',' she reminded me.
How I wish now that I'd accompanied her on some of her self-
styled adventures, instead of only ever spending time with her at
home in her cottage. I'm sure I could have had the opportunity, if
only I'd asked her. I could have gone on to write books about the
pleasures of travelling with my aunt.

Or I could have been Henry Pulling to Aunt Augusta – the
staid, unadventurous nephew given a new perspective on life by
his aged relation, according to the blurb on the back of the
Graham Greene book that Hector had given me earlier.

The realisation of what now would never be made my eyes fill
with tears and my heart heave with shame at my ingratitude. I
wiped my damp hands on the soft velvet of May's long skirt, now
hugging my legs. I continued to stroke it long after my hands
were dry.

* * *

I started reading *Travels with My Aunt* that evening with a glass of wine in a hot bath, seasoned with Auntie May's favourite lily of the valley bath salts. After twice dropping the book in the bath, I climbed out, slipped on my nightie and hung the book on the washing line in the garden to dry. Then I decided to reacquaint myself with May's own books in bed.

Even without the bookshop in the village, there was plenty to read in May's cottage. It was jammed full of books, including copies translated into different languages. I used to lie in bed, staring at the black and white photos of her waving from the back of a camel, lounging in a hammock in the tropics, or strolling round the deck of an ocean-going liner. It was hard to equate the lithe, sporty figure in sola topi and shorts with the bent old lady that I knew, but when I read her writing, she seemed forever young.

I hated to confess, even to myself, that I hadn't opened any of her books since I used to stay as a teenager. I wondered how much different they'd seem now I was reading them with an adult perspective.

I was about to reach for the special shelf in her bedroom where she kept a first edition of each of her books when I noticed the green Moleskine notebook that I'd spotted the night before. I'd left it where it was, nervous of intruding on Auntie May's personal space. Emboldened now by having a job and feeling a little more like I belonged here, I picked it up and opened it, expecting to find a poignant final diary entry, written the last night she spent in her own bed. Instead I discovered the book was entirely empty, apart from a note on the first page addressed to me in her familiar, neat sloping curling hand.

'My dear Sophie, whatever you do, live a life worth writing down. Then write it down. Ever with you, Auntie May'.

I gazed at her message. Could I really do that in this village?

'Write what you know,' they say. But what did I know? How to teach English to foreign students? Or how to get bogged down in a disastrous dead-end relationship? Not much inspiration there.

The thought made me gladder than ever that I'd landed the job in the bookshop. It would buy me time to reconsider, even though I wasn't entirely sure it would cover my bills. Although I had no rent, I'd still have to pay council tax, and for electricity, food and transport. And I didn't have so much as a pushbike, so probably ought to buy a car. And learn to drive.

With a start, I realised that Hector hadn't mentioned the rate of pay, and I hadn't asked. Maybe he wanted a free intern, happy to make do with only the tips from the tearoom. That would explain why he'd been so fast to appoint me.

What had begun as a simple proposition – to live in a rent-free cottage, in a pleasant, stable community, while pursuing the writing ambitions that I'd held since childhood – now seemed fraught with traps, difficulties and dangers. I put down the diary gently on the nightstand and settled back to sleep, curled up beneath Auntie May's ancient Indian silk counterpane, savouring the sounds and scents of the village drifting in through the open bedroom window, and trying to cast my worries from my mind.

9

THE CREAM OF THE BOOKSHOP

I awoke refreshed, reminded for the second night in a row how comfortable feather beds are. Leaping up to make a cup of tea, I then took it back to bed to drink while I read *The Bookseller*. I thought it would put me in the right frame of mind for my first day as a bookshop assistant. From its pages, I planned to pick up the trade's jargon quickly and so impress upon Hector that he had hired the right person.

An hour later, I wondered with a start what a giant moth was doing on my face. It was *The Bookseller*, open at pages two to three, sticking to the corner of my mouth where I'd dribbled slightly in my sleep. Peeling it off, I set it to one side on the counterpane and reached for my mug of tea, now stone cold, so it was clearly time to get up. May's clock revealed that I'd slept through my alarm.

I threw on the clothes I'd had the foresight to lay out ready the night before – I'd selected my own leggings and an arty Indian silk tunic of Auntie May's – and was in and out of the bathroom within five minutes. Then, chewing on a dried-up scone as a token gesture at breakfast, I ran up the High Street. I arrived at Hector's House just as he was turning the 'Closed' sign to 'Open'. I tried not to pant as I crossed the threshold, as if I'd strolled up leisurely, on time, and in control.

Hector, not fooled for a moment, looked pointedly at his watch. 'The school mums will be with us any minute for their post-school-run revivers.'

'You mean the alcoholic tea?' I asked, heading for the tearoom area and looking about me for clues as to what I was meant to do next.

Hector looked askance. 'No! Not at 9 a.m.! What do you take them for? Or me? Only Billy starts that early.'

I felt embarrassed at my blunder until he continued.

'No, save that for when they really need it – when they've collected the children in the afternoon.'

Making up my new routine as I went along, I gave the three tin tables a quick wipe with a damp cloth and laid them up with sugar bowls and newly-filled milk jugs. There was no room on the tiny tables for menus, so the choices were chalked up on a blackboard beside the cake counter. The glass domes that had yesterday guarded cakes now enclosed nothing but air. I replenished them with the contents of a couple of Tupperware boxes that had been left on the counter, presumably delivered that morning by Mrs Wetherley. Then I set out teapots, cups and saucers ready for the first customers.

I'd just set the lid down on the last pot when the first of the mums entered the shop. Hector clicked on some relaxing New Age music as a soothing soundtrack after the frenetic school run – the perfect antidote to children's breakfast television jingles. Soon half a dozen ladies were clustered round the tables, drinking the pots of tea I'd served them and tucking into Mrs Wetherley's cakes. I gathered this was their breakfast. It was more mouth-watering than mine.

My presence appeared to surprise them. Perhaps they were

disappointed to be served by me rather than the handsome Hector. Said bookseller was making the most of his new freedom by lounging behind the shop counter, typing something into the computer. I'd always assumed that the only thing booksellers did when they weren't selling books to customers was to read them.

'Haven't I seen you somewhere before?' asked a lady cuddling a small baby girl with one hand while picking at a cupcake with the other. 'You look familiar.'

'I used to spend some of my holidays here when I was a teenager.'

'No, I only moved here four years ago.'

I sighed. 'You'll be thinking of my aunt, then.'

She brightened. 'Oh yes, old May Sayers down the road. You're really like her. So sad, poor May, dying like that. Still, to be expected at her age, I suppose.'

I explained how she'd left me her cottage, enabling me to start a new life as a writer in the village after four years of travel. I hoped she might assume my itinerary had been as exotic as my aunt's.

'Have you always worked in bookshops?'

'No, but I'm glad to be working here now. I used to be an English teacher, working overseas.'

'An English teacher?' one of the other mums on the next table chipped in. 'Do you do coaching? My Jemima really could do with some extra help with her reading.'

'I'm afraid my special subject is English as a Foreign Language, not literacy.'

'It might as well be a foreign language, Jemima's that bad at it. Would you consider giving her some extra help after school anyway? No-one else offers coaching in this village. I'm happy to pay the going rate.'

I glanced over to Hector to check whether he was listening.

There'd still been no talk of my pay. I wondered whether to accept.

'The thing is, I've just started working here now.' I spoke loudly, so Hector would hear. 'So I'll be in here every afternoon when the children come out of school.'

Hector hit 'enter' decisively and looked up from his keyboard.

'Here's a plan,' he said with a winning smile to the mothers. 'Sophie will coach your children here after school. She can use the desk in the stock room while you enjoy a cup of tea, a bun and a good book here. That will save you going home and coming back at the start and finish of each lesson.'

'And if the children work hard, you could buy them a cake or a biscuit afterwards,' I added. 'I'm free any afternoon that suits you.'

Before I knew it, we had three pupils scheduled on alternate weekdays and the promise of more interest from their friends. After the mums had headed off to take their younger children to playgroup at the Village Hall, I scooped up the tips from beneath the saucers. I wondered whether there'd ever been a more brazen moonlighter.

'Well done, Sophie, that was entrepreneurial of you,' said Hector.

'I didn't do anything. It was all down to you.'

'Not at all. You've just got us some extra tearoom business, created another vital role in the community for the shop, and boosted your salary to boot.'

I wasn't comfortable taking all the credit. I wondered how to repay him for his kindness.

'If I need any special books for teaching purposes, I'll order them through the shop.'

'What teamwork! At least now I can stop feeling guilty for paying you minimum wage, as you'll be topping it up with teaching fees. Even if it is multitasking, of which, as a man, I have to disapprove on principle.'

I had a sudden panic. 'Are you sure it's not illegal?'

'Not if you fill in the right forms for child protection. I do know about health and safety, you know. I'm not completely irresponsible.'

* * *

The rest of the morning continued less eventfully, with Hector serving a few customers who came in to collect specific orders, and directing a couple of browsers in search of postable presents. After a while, I began to spot a pattern.

'How is it that every time you see a new customer coming, you change the track on the music player?' I'd been enjoying the violin quartet that had accompanied the visit of an elderly man. Hector had despatched him with a copy of John Galsworthy's *Forsyte Saga*.

Hector looked pleased with himself. 'All part of the olde worlde bookshop charm. Makes a customer feel comfortable and at home, and when they're relaxed, so are their purse strings. Next on my playlist will be the dulcet tones of the local silver band. What better overture to the Village Show Committee meeting, due here at midday?'

He must have thought I was looking blank. 'Haven't you ever been here for the Village Show?'

'No. It falls at the end of the summer, and I had to be back at school in Scotland in mid-August, so I always missed it.'

Hector looked genuinely sorry for me. 'You'll see for yourself in a couple of months what it's all about. In the meantime, do your best to keep the Show Committee sweet. I sell the Show programmes in here all through the summer, and often flog a few books to people who come in for them, so I'd be loath to lose them. I order in seasonal gardening books especially, to help local gardeners boost their chances of winning a prize. The Committee puts a lot of business through the tearoom too. I'll show you before they get here where I keep the cream – the special cream that Billy likes so much. But for now, could you cut along to the village shop and buy a couple more pints of milk? We'll be needing them.'

After the cool atmosphere of Hector's House, stepping out onto the hot pavement in my sandals, I was reminded that we were approaching midsummer. I strolled slowly along the road to the village shop, where I found Carol fanning herself with a copy of the parish magazine.

'So tell me about the Village Show,' I said casually as I searched out the milk in the chiller cabinet, where it lay between the ham and the pasties. I set the milk cartons down on the counter so as to fish my purse out of my pocket. 'What happens? And what's so special about it?'

Carol looked at me as if I'd just beamed down from another planet. She needed no further prompting to share her enthusiasm.

'Oh, the *Show*! The Show's the best day of the whole year. There's a huge marquee for everyone's competition fruit, flowers, vegetables and crafts, and a funfair, and a carnival parade in fancy dress down the High Street. And entertainments in the arena – we had sheepdog demonstrations last year, and a falconer, and some nice young gymnasts come up from Slate Green with terrific acrostic skills. Then there's the tug-of-war and the tractor pull and the Morris Men and the rare breeds and—'

'A busy afternoon, then?'

'Not just an afternoon. It goes into the evening too, because the beer tent remains open till it's been drunk dry. Which is one reason why the auction of all the goods at the end of the night makes so much profit. And you'll need to be up at the crack of dawn to get your entries into the judging tent before the ten o'clock bell. Make sure you save your pennies for the Show, Sophie, because it's a really good day out. People come from miles around to see it, and everyone in the village takes part. What will you enter in the show? You've got to enter something. Are you any good at baking cakes? Preserves? Chutneys? Wines?'

I felt inadequate. 'No, not at all. To recognise my level of skill in the kitchen, they'd have to have a category for toast.'

'How about the best salad on a plate? You don't have to grow it or cook it, of course. Just make a pretty arrangement. Or you can enter eggs or honey if you keep chickens or bees, though technically speaking it's not you who produces them. Joshua, next door to you, has won the best honey in show award for the last three years. Your auntie often took the cup for best photo, with the snaps she captured while she was away in exotic places on her travels. What's your special talent? I'm sure you must have one.'

She gave my hand an encouraging pat as she pressed the change and the receipt into my palm, clearly no more convinced than I was that I had spectacular skills to display.

'What about writing?' I ventured gingerly. 'Is there a prize for writing?'

'Best handwriting for their age, but only for the under-twelves.'

'Not that sort of writing. Creative writing.'

'I tell you what.' She leaned forward across the counter conspiratorially. 'Why don't you ask the Committee to add a new category for your sort of writing? They reconsider the programme every year, adding new classes to move with the times. They even have prizes for digital photos now. And the new loom band jewellery class was oversubscribed last year. Though I doubt it will be this year.'

She indicated a basket on the corner of the counter. There languished a few dozen packs of loom bands, marked down successively from £1 to 50p to 10p per pack, and still not shifting.

'Brilliant idea, Carol!'

'And a new category might not attract many entries, giving you a better chance of winning a prize. Funny that nobody's thought of it before, really, what with there being a village writers' group.'

This was news to me. I felt absurdly disappointed that my aunt and I were not the only writers in the village.

'Was May in it?'

'She gave them the odd pep talk, I think, but none of them were in her league. They're not proper writers, like her. Most of them haven't published anything yet. But I bet they'd give it a go. Run the idea past the Show Committee to see what they think. Worst that can happen is that they say no.'

The Show Committee! I'd forgotten all about them. I grabbed the milk cartons that I was meant to be taking urgently for their tea.

'Who exactly is on the Show Committee? Anyone I might know? Anyone who is particularly keen on literature or the clever use of words?'

'Well, there's Billy,' she said brightly, following me to the door to turn the 'Open' sign to 'Closed' for her lunch break. I left the shop, the doorbell jangling heavily in the humid afternoon heat, and returned to Hector's House to tackle the Show Committee with sinking heart. I had the distinct feeling that this might not end well.

10

THE SHOW COMMITTEE

I strolled back down the High Street clutching a large carton of milk to my chest to cool me down in the midday heat. In my absence, a strange array of vehicles had congregated outside Hector's House. This included a mud-spattered off-road tricycle, now very much on the road; a small rusting tractor; two ancient bicycles; and a navy blue Nissan Micra. Pushing open the door, I was struck by the impression that the tearoom was entirely full, even though only five people sat there. Hector made the introductions, as Billy, who possessed one of the bikes, was the only face familiar to me.

I learned that Stanley Harding, a stout middle-aged man in checked flannel shirt and ancient twill trousers, was the third-generation Show Committee Chairman. He had come by tractor, not wanting to lose time getting back to the fields afterwards. Trevor Jenkins, a dusty-looking builder of about forty, had come on the tricycle. He'd off-roaded across the recreation ground from his current building site: an infill home by an old barn at the edge of the village. Bob Blake, the community policeman, had come on the shinier of the bikes, and was still wearing his bicycle clips.

Tilly Westman, local nurse and owner of the Micra, was smiling encouragingly at me from under her long, straight mousey fringe. I suspected she was glad of another female presence to offset the testosterone.

She patted an empty seat beside her. 'Welcome aboard, Sophie. Hector's been telling us what a good ideas person you are, and that you are keen to join the Show Committee. We could certainly do with some fresh blood.'

Whose blood were they about to spill?

'I hadn't been planning to join the Committee—' I began, casting a pleading glance at Hector. He simply nodded and waved his hand towards the chair, indicating that I should sit down. I took comfort from sitting opposite a policeman.

Hector turned away and continued taking books out of a large cardboard carton, scanning their barcodes and putting them on the shelves. He looked as if he was shopping in reverse.

'Don't get too comfortable till you've served up our tea, young miss,' objected Billy, waving in the direction of the cake counter. 'Your special tea, by the way.'

When I got up to flick the switch on the kettle, Hector set down his barcode scanner and sidled over to me casually, standing very close. He opened a door concealed beneath the counter and lifted out an unlabelled bottle of an opaque liquid and pressed it into my hand. It looked like off-white emulsion paint.

'You'll find the special cream for Billy's jug in here, Sophie.' He lifted out a new bottle. 'I dare say the others will sneak a splash too.'

Once the tea was made and the cream was flowing, I quickly discovered the various roles within the Committee. Bob was Entries Secretary, making sure that all entrants submitted their produce for display with the right paperwork filled in. Trevor managed the events, providing the hay bales needed for seating around the edge of the arena and constructing the marquee and beer tent. From the size of his tummy, I suspected he was also its best customer. As well as chairing the Committee, Stan provided the pig for the hog roast and the farm hands to turn the spit and carve the meat. Billy was Prizes Officer, organising the champions' trophies. Tilly was the Show Secretary, generally providing common sense and order, and managing all the correspondence. She also created the Show Programme, which, as luck would have it, was the main purpose of the day's meeting. She passed us each a copy of the previous year's edition: a twelve-page stapled leaflet.

'So today we need to look at ways of boosting the carnival parade, because we get fewer trailer floats each year,' began Stanley. 'Plenty of walkers in costume, but not so many people willing to enter floats. I can't think why.'

I hesitated to intervene so early, but I didn't want to miss this chance to make my mark. 'Maybe there aren't so many farmers with trailers available as there used to be. Or, indeed, so many farmers.'

A murmur went around the table.

'I'm buggered if she ain't spot on there,' Billy spluttered, putting his teacup down with such a crash that I surreptitiously looked for cracks in the china. 'Three of the farmers who used to tow floats each year had been unfortunately harvested by their maker before last year's show.'

Trying to suppress a grisly vision of farmers tumbling into their own threshing machines, I needed a long draught of my tea before I could speak again. Then I realised Billy was speaking metaphorically. A translator would come in handy round here, I thought.

'I think what Sophie is suggesting,' said Tilly, kindly, 'is that we need to persuade some newcomers to put floats in.'

'You can't rustle up a trailer if you haven't got one,' argued Bob. 'Besides, most of the new houses don't have enough parking space to take a trailer, even if people have got a tow bar on their cars.'

'Parking space, my arse,' replied Billy, in the best non sequitur I'd heard for a while. 'They've all got bloody four by fours, and if all they need is a trailer, Stan here can find one for them – can't you, boy? You've got plenty of rusting trailers lying about unused in the old barn by your woods.'

Stanley hesitated. 'I think I have two, if people are prepared to decorate them and they're willing to come down to my land to do it. But who would we ask?'

'Playgroup and the WI are all sorted already, and Gardening Club's using my flatbed truck,' said Trevor.

'There are plenty of organisations in the village,' said Tilly. 'But I don't know how we persuade them to do it. Everyone's so busy planning their holidays in the run-up to the Show.'

The answer seemed obvious to me. 'Tell them it would be a great way to promote their particular clubs. It would help them recruit new members, or promote any events that they're planning for later in the year.'

'Wendlebury Players,' put in Tilly. 'They'll be doing an autumn show, and it would help sell tickets. They're always looking for new male members.'

Billy sniggered.

'And new women too, now,' added Trevor, 'because so many of them left after the *Sound of Music* casting fiasco. All the best actresses, anyway.'

'They're all big bloody show-offs,' said Billy. 'A load of middle-aged women happy to flaunt themselves in public. That Linda Absolom is the worst of the lot.'

Hector heckled from behind the shop counter, where he sat bashing away at his computer keyboard. 'Not something you normally complain about, Billy.'

'Or we could ask the Wendlebury Writers,' said Tilly. 'They're very creative. Some women might be in both, though. That might be a problem.'

'Some women are in every bloody group in the village,' said Billy. 'Old busybodies.'

Stanley knew how to rein him back in. 'And you are on how many committees, Billy? Four, is it now? Or five, including the Gardening Club?'

'If you want something done, you know what they say.' Unperturbed, Billy poured himself another cup of tea.

'I'll minute that we'll offer Stanley's two trailers to the Wendlebury Writers and the Wendlebury Players,' said Tilly, scribbling on her shorthand pad. 'Who's that an action point for, then?'

There was an ominous silence, while they all looked at each other, then at me.

'You're the only one on the Committee who hasn't got any jobs to do at the moment,' said Billy. 'Get a grip, girlie.'

He put his hands together in an illustrative gesture that made me imagine him wringing my neck.

Hector let out a bark of laughter. 'Yes, come on, Sophie, get a grip.'

My eyes fixed on Billy's curled hands, I found myself nodding eagerly as Tilly minuted my acceptance. Stanley ran his finger down to the next point on the agenda.

'Right, now that's sorted, we need to review all the classes for entries, add new ones in and remove any for which there were not enough entries last year to justify sustaining them.' He opened his copy of the previous year's show programme and bent it right back at the spine, as if loosening it up for some serious physical action.

After poring over eight pages of entry classes, we all came up for air and a long draught of tea. Billy drained his cup and refilled it, topping it up with a generous tot of cream.

'I don't think we'll need a loom band category this year,' suggested the sensible Tilly, tapping the point of her pen against the children's section. 'They were a one-summer wonder. I'm not sure what has taken their place this year. If any child is behind the times and is still making them, they can enter one under the Any Other Handicraft section.'

'Agreed.' Bob struck it from the list with a short, stubby pencil. 'And I think everyone's had enough of the potato wine class, after all the sickness it caused last year. I know I couldn't face another drop. I'm entering the potatoes from my allotment this year just as potatoes.'

'An imaginative lot, our boys in blue,' murmured Billy.

'I think it's time to add knitting in three and four ply back in again,' suggested Tilly. 'I've seen several small children in delicate little cardies in the playpark this summer. I don't know who's making them, but they're definitely hand knits.'

'Any other ideas for new categories?' asked Stan, flicking through the programme again. 'Anything else to freshen up the mix? Billy?'

'Whittling, say I. Nothing wrong with a bit of whittling. Or knife-sharpening, now there's a real art.'

I really didn't want to see Billy with a sharp knife in his hands, whether for whittling or any other purpose.

I cleared my throat. 'Actually, I was wondering about a writing competition. No, not handwriting' – Trevor was stabbing pointedly at the children's section – 'but creative writing, for adults. You know, poems or travelogues or short stories.' They looked dubious. 'I'd love to have the chance to enter a short story competition.'

There was a silence, broken by Stan. 'Maybe you could endow a trophy in honour of your late aunt?' He held up his programme, open at the list of trophies, each named after a dead person. There was a Henry Snow Giant Parsnip Cup, the Albert Beetle Beetroot Medal, the Shirley Salisbury Woolly Jumper Trophy (I wasn't clear whether the latter one was for knitting or for training sheep). 'How about the May Sayers Golden Inkwell?'

'Endow means you pay for it,' Tilly added, to be clear.

'We could award it for best limerick,' piped up Billy, now on his fourth cup of tea. 'I wouldn't mind having a go at that one myself: there once was a woman named May, always up for a roll in the hay—'

Bob wagged an admonishing finger at him. 'Now, now, Billy, show a bit of respect for them as has lost her. In any case, it's not as if May Sayers wrote limericks, is it?'

'She might have done. On her days off.' Billy looked hurt, but then he brightened. 'Maybe we could make it that all the limericks have to be about May Sayers, out of respect. Shouldn't be hard, as her name's an easy one to rhyme with. As is my own: a handsome old farmer named Billy, was renowned for the size of his—'

'Yes, that's enough of that, William.'

Stanley tried in vain to silence him, but Billy was apparently on a roll.

'Sophie, now that's much trickier—'

I was glad when Tilly interrupted him. 'Trophy. Sophie and Trophy. So are you happy to pay for the trophy, Sophie?'

'As her next of kin, I suppose it would be down to me. Which is absolutely fine, by the way, if you tell me how to go about ordering one. I've never done anything like this before.'

Hector left his computer to come and stand behind me. 'Actually, Hector's House would be honoured to fund a trophy in May Sayers's memory. It would remind people to come into my shop to buy her books. Sophie, what do you think it should be for – poetry, travel writing or a broader topic?'

I was keen to move in the direction of prose, as I've never been able to dream up rhymes to save my life. I've always believed there's a poetry gene, like the gene which determines whether or not you're good at doing foreign accents. I have neither.

'Like the classic school essay, 'What I Did in My Holidays', only for grown-ups?' asked Bob, frowning as if trying to rack his brains for something memorable from his own last trip away.

'She was a traveller, not a tourist,' I said gently, not wanting to hurt the policeman's feelings. It seemed a good idea to stay on the right side of the law.

'I know! Nature writing!' put in Stanley. 'So as not to show prejudice against those as don't travel anywhere. A nice bit of nature writing about our village pond, perhaps, or the valley down yonder. Or anywhere that takes your fancy, really.'

'*Down yonder green valley, where streamlets meander,*' sang Bob in a light tenor.

Billy looked impressed. 'Very good, our copper. I wouldn't have put you down for the poetic type.'

Tilly set him straight. 'Oh, Billy, Bob didn't make that up. It's an old traditional song. Have you never heard of *The Ash Grove*?'

'That's the pub up Moreton way, isn't it?' Billy poured himself another cup of tea. For a moment I had an irresistible urge to try to cram his whole body into the teapot to silence him, like the dormouse at the Mad Hatter's Tea Party.

'Nature writing it is, then,' concluded Stanley. 'Not too long a piece, mind, so the judges have time to read them all. Could be a long job if we have too many entries in. How long do you reckon, Sophie?'

I was pleased he regarded me as the writing expert in the room. 'How about 250 words? That's roughly enough to fill one side of A4. And who should judge?'

I wanted to deflect that role away from myself so that I wouldn't be excluded from entering. Billy lobbed a sugar lump at Hector. His aim was surprisingly sharp.

'Hector, you old bugger, are you up to judging some writing about nature?'

'Now, Billy, ladies present,' said Stanley, chivalrously.

'Oh, all right, then – Hector, you old sod.'

Hector dusted granules of sugar off his shirt. 'Can't be me, anyway. Needs to be someone from beyond the village, as well you know. Why not get one of the Slate Green secondary school teachers? Not Rex or Julia, of course, because although they teach there, they live in the village. But they might invite their head of English to volunteer.'

'Minuted,' said Tilly, scribbling on her pad. 'I'll ask Julia.'

'Quite right too,' muttered Billy. 'We don't want that good-for-nothing Rex getting involved. I don't trust that old devil more than I could throw him. And I reckons I could throw him further than you might think.'

He rolled up the grubby sleeve of his shirt and flexed a surprisingly muscly forearm on the table, as if about to challenge one of us to a round of arm-wrestling. It could prove dangerous if combined with his sharpened whittling knife. I hoped he'd left it at home.

Stanley ignored Billy and turned to me. 'Sophie, I suggest you pay a visit to the Wendlebury Writers when they meet in The Bluebird tomorrow to tell them about the new writing cup. Ask them to put in a float too, while you're at it. Then next Tuesday evening the Wendlebury Players are having a meeting in the Village Hall about their next production, so you can go and buttonhole them about their float.'

'Why would they do what I tell them?' I queried. My past experience with actors had not filled me with confidence.

'For one thing, they'll take notice of the new Assistant Entries Secretary,' he said. 'Everyone in favour of Sophie's appointment, I take it? Good, carried unanimously!' Tilly added my name to the list of Committee members inside the front cover of her minute book. 'And for another thing, you'll be offering the writers the chance to display their golden words to the world at large. As to the Players, Rex is a pushover for a pretty girl like you. And what Rex says, the women in the Wendlebury Players will do. It's like he's got hypnotic powers.'

'Those women that are left,' put in Billy.

'Well, he did used to be a conjuror, Stanley,' said Tilly. I wondered whether she'd ever fallen under Rex's spell. 'But it doesn't always last. There's been a steady trail of departures from the Wendlebury Players since Rex took over as director last year.'

Billy looked thoughtful. 'I could do with Rex teaching me a few tricks with the ladies,' he began, but was silenced by a sharp look from Stanley. I could see why Stanley was the Chairman.

* * *

After they'd all left, I turned accusingly on Hector.

'How on earth did that happen? I don't remember volunteering to join the Show Committee.'

Hector smirked. 'Oh, you don't have to volunteer to be co-opted on to village committees. Newcomers find themselves doing all sorts of things they didn't mean to once they've been here a while.'

Silently I hoped that didn't include murder. He misinterpreted the look of horror on my face.

'If you don't want to join in the fun, you'll need to learn how to put up more of a fight before they close in on you. Anyway, they probably won't make you do much first time round, especially if you're going to join the Writers, because you'll be on a float. You'll just be in reserve in case Bob gets hit by a tractor or something.'

Did he mean by accident or murderous intention? My voice came out a little shrill. 'Does that happen often in these parts?'

He shook his head, and his winning smile overcame my resistance. I got on with clearing away the tea things to the accompaniment of a medley of English folk songs. As I did so, I started planning my approach to the Wendlebury Writers. I hoped they weren't much good. I didn't want my writing shown up.

Hanging the tea towel up to dry, I served a young woman who had come in to buy a birthday card. Then I wandered over to the stationery shelf, entirely stocked by the Literally Gifted company, and selected a few items to lend myself an air of writerly experience at the meeting the next evening.

As I left the shop to go home at five o'clock, Hector slipped a slim book into the 'Books Are My Bag' bag that I'd found hanging over the back of Auntie May's desk chair. I withdrew it for inspection once I reached my garden gate: *The Elements of Style*. For a moment, I thought it must be a fashion guide, assuming he hadn't liked today's artistic tunic, but I opened the book to discover a definitive guide for writers.

I had to say this for Hector: he was nothing if not kind. I wondered if our growing friendship might work in my favour at the Village Show, fervently hoping that neither of us would be hit by a tractor or skewered by a sharpened whittling knife in the meantime.

'Why have you been so kind to me, Hector?'

On my second day working at Hector's House, while slipping some used printer paper into the waste paper box in the store room, I discovered a pile of completed application forms for the assistant's job. All had been submitted the week before I arrived back in the village. At the top of each one was a brief note in Hector's looping handwriting, summarising the merits and demerits of the candidate. Three of them bore favourable comments, and all of them lived in the village.

'What do you mean, Sophie?' Hector looked up from his keyboard for a moment, fixing me with his green-eyed gaze. 'I'm kind to everyone. What makes you think I've singled you out for special treatment?'

I stepped out of the stockroom doorway, wiggled my way around the tearoom tables, and produced the pile of discarded CVs with a flourish from behind my back. As I spread them on the wooden counter in front of Hector, he minimised the screen into which he'd been typing hard for the last twenty minutes.

'You told me no-one else had applied for the job when you took me on.'

He turned his gaze to the window, pretending to consider. 'Really? What I meant was, no-one else local.'

'Oh, Hector, that's not true! These are nearly all from villagers. Why are you doing this? Anyway, I have yet to see why you need an assistant. There's only a trickle of visitors all day, apart from the tea trade, and never a queue. Hardly enough to justify two salaries, even if you're paying us both minimum wage.'

Hector got up from his stool, swept the CVs into a neat pile, and then tore them easily in half. I wondered how he'd be with telephone directories.

'That's what you get for snooping. Confused. Misinformed. False conclusions.' He sighed. 'Make us both a latte and I'll tell you why.'

He took the ripped CVs out to the stockroom, and as I frothed the milk I heard him tearing them into smaller pieces before dumping them back in the paper recycling box. He returned to settle on one of the tearoom chairs as I set a tall glass of coffee in front of him. Then I pulled out the seat opposite and sat down with one for myself.

'Okay, so perhaps I wasn't telling the whole truth. What I should have said was, no-one else applied who was the niece of Miss May Sayers.'

'You make it sound like she was a member of the Mafia, as if she had some hold over you.'

Hector stirred the latte with a long-handled spoon, dispersing the cocoa powder I'd sprinkled on the top. 'She sort of did, only not intentionally. You see, May Sayers was very supportive when I first set up the bookshop. She was a close friend of my parents, and she knew when they retired that antiques were not my thing. I'd always worked in bookshops since university, and even at uni,

and she knew how much I loved them. She helped me persuade
my parents that converting the shop for my preferred purpose
was a good idea. In return, I let her choose its name. How was I to
know she was especially fond of a 1960s television puppet show
about a dog called Hector? Still, if that was the worst of my
mistakes, I wasn't doing so badly.

'I had no capital, only the premises, which my parents gifted
to me. The deal was that it was down to me to raise the money to
buy my initial stock, and your aunt kindly gave me a personal
loan to set me up. She also gave me lots of her own books to sell,
every time she had spare author copies from her publisher. She's
always been one of my two bestselling authors, given her local
profile.'

'Who's the other one?' I asked, thinking there was another
author that I didn't know about lurking in the village.

Hector scraped back his chair and headed over to the modern
fiction shelves, where he picked up a thick paperback with a pale
lavender cover featuring a young blonde woman burying her face
in a bunch of sweet peas.

'Hermione Minty,' I read off the cover when he passed me the
book. I flipped it over to read the blurb. 'I've heard of her, of
course. But she's not local, is she?'

'There's no-one Minty in this village, unless they've just
cleaned their teeth. But she's prolific, and her romances fly off the
shelves. That's why I always have her full range in stock, an
honour not granted to many authors by bookshops.'

'You've got a couple in the window too, I noticed.' I hoped this
might score me some points.

'So there you go,' said Hector. 'My secret's out. May Sayers
helped get my business off the ground, and I never found a way to
repay her kindness while she was alive. I'd repaid the loan in full,

I hasten to add, by the end of my first two years of trading, but she refused to let me pay her any interest.'

'But you stock all her books.' I admired the beautiful display he'd made of them against a background of vintage maps in the travel section.

'Yes, but they more than pay the rent on their shelf space, and I make good money from her work, so she's still doing me favours from beyond the grave. So when you pitched up, I felt as if I had a golden opportunity to repay her in kind.'

I stared into my coffee, trying to take this news in. 'I'm sure she'd approve,' I said eventually. 'Of what we're both doing.'

Hector gave a gentle smile. 'Yes, I'm sure she'd approve of us both.'

In the distance, the school bell clanged, and Hector got up from his chair. 'So, enough gossip for now. Jump to it. The after-school rush will be with us in a minute.' Already some mums with pushchairs were heading past the shop towards the school gate. 'Back to work, Miss Sayers, before you stretch my good nature to its limits. And don't forget, after that, you've got a Wendlebury Writers meeting to prepare for.'

I whisked his empty mug away to the sink, feeling that I had landed on my feet. I could hardly believe my good fortune, all of it attributable to Auntie May's generosity. Yet somehow everything seemed to be falling into place too easily. I couldn't help thinking that there must be a catch, and I wasn't looking forward to finding out what it was.

12

WRITERS AFLOAT

It wasn't hard to spot the Wendlebury Writers in the pub. They were gathered around a circular table in the bay window, three of them sitting on the curved oak window seat, four more on rickety old cane-seated wooden chairs. All had ring binders or notebooks in front of them. Discovering they were all women startled me. I'd assumed that they would be roughly half men and half women. No chance of recruiting a new boyfriend here.

They all looked up as I came towards them from the bar, where I'd bought a glass of Dutch courage.

'Hello, you're Sophie, aren't you?' said a slim, pale woman with cropped dark hair. She stood up to drag a stool across from a nearby empty table and gestured to it invitingly. 'Here you go. I'm Dinah, and I'm the Chair.'

'But don't sit on her!'

The voice from the bar was familiar.

'Hello, Billy.' I gave him a little wave, thinking it best to keep on the right side of him after his surprising show of strength and interest in sharp knives at the Show Committee meeting.

Dinah ignored him. 'Don't worry, we haven't started without you.'

'How did you know I was coming?'

'Billy told me when I arrived,' said Dinah.

'Oh, really? Carol told me when I called in for my prescription earlier,' said a woman about my age in an old-fashioned thin pink cardigan.

'I found out from Hector,' added a middle-aged lady in a floral cotton shirtwaister: the sort from catalogues for the age group that embraces elastic waistbands. To be more accurate, it was actually a shirtwaistless, but at least its shades of cornflower and forget-me-not blue suited her blonde colouring nicely. 'I bumped into him at the allotments, when I went to pick some salad leaves for my tea. But the ground was like concrete, and I couldn't pull a lettuce.'

There was a chortle from the bar. 'Couldn't pull a lettuce, eh? A bit like young Hector. Poor lonely young Hector.'

'I notice you never say a word against Hector when you're ensconced in his shop, Billy,' said Donald the publican, wiping the bar with a towel.

Billy growled something unintelligible into his beer.

'So, we all seem to know you already,' continued Dinah. 'Or at least we know who you are and where you live. Why don't you tell us a bit about your writing?'

She put her hands on her strong jodhpured thighs and leaned back expectantly. To my relief, another member of the group came to my rescue while I was still floundering for what to say. I hadn't really expected an inquisition.

'Now, Dinah, don't put the poor girl on the spot,' said the slim woman in pink. 'Why don't we go round the table and say a line or two about ourselves to set the ball rolling for her?'

Dinah thumped a bright orange charity collection box on the table. It was labelled 'Readathon – Reading for Life'.

'Cliché alert! 10p, please, Karen.'

Karen fished a coin out of her purse and dropped it into the slot. 'Sorry, Dinah. I'm Karen, and I write short stories for women's magazines..'

She looked to her left, to the shirtwaistless lady.

'I'm Louisa, and I'm interested in writing detective stories, in the style of the Golden Age of crime fiction. I've had a few false starts, so I'm currently reading the complete works of the Queen of Crime herself, in the order in which she wrote them. I couldn't wish for a better teacher.'

She clasped her hands together and emitted a little sigh of satisfaction.

'Gosh, that's a lot of books to get through,' I ventured. 'How far have you got?'

'Ooh, about halfway. I'm learning so much. I'm hoping to start writing by 2020.'

'I'm Dinah,' cut in the pale lady, apparently forgetting she'd already told me her name. 'I write literary fiction with strong female protagonists. There aren't enough of those around. Nor enough strong female writers either. Far too many who won't even admit their sex in their name. As if the androgyny of J K Rowling wasn't enough, she's now calling herself by a man's name, Robert Galbraith.'

'You must admit, Dinah, it doesn't stop her selling billions of books.' This came from a woman with dark hair in an expensive and intriguing asymmetrical cut, which made her look as if she'd gone to a sculptor rather than a hairdresser. She went on to introduce herself as Jacky, the local dentist interested in writing her memoirs, tentatively entitled *Dental Records*. She hoped none of her patients would recognise themselves and sue her – she'd posted a few tales on her blog about the misadventures of a dentist, written in the third person and changing the names and settings, but still people claimed that the incidents described were about them. 'The funny thing is, those stories were entirely made up. I would never share actual case studies.'

Next to Jacky sat Jessica, a lady in black leggings and a volu-minous black smock, liberally scattered with white dog hair. I suspected her pockets contained a stash of dog biscuits. She explained that she wrote sweet poems about animals and was happy to take commissions for birthdays and Christmases. When she asked hopefully about my dog's birthday, she was disap-pointed to find me petless. Her own dog lay beneath the table, wedged cosily between the wall and its owner's ankles, tail occa-sionally thudding contentedly.

'I write poetry too,' volunteered Bella, a lady of about sixty in a timeless linen shift dress that made her look cool as a cucumber (damn, another 10p gone, at least in my head. Good thing I wasn't saying much out loud). 'But more about nature than animals.'

'You can't get much more natural than cats and dogs,' protested Jessica.

'Not when they're bred to the point of illness,' said Dinah brusquely.

'Nature in its elemental state, then.' Bella added that she was the Parish Clerk and the wife of the local GP, as if that were rele-vant to what she wrote. All it did was explain to me how she managed to be unperturbed by Dinah's aggression. She was clearly used to dealing with powerful, influential people and putting them back in their box.

I had never noticed before this meeting how many clichés I used.

'I'm the only historical fiction writer in the group,' said a lady with grey closely-cropped hair. Her name was Julia. 'I'm a history teacher by day, and a historical novelist by night. I specialise in the Tudor period, but these days we have to teach anything and everything the government tells us, and not necessarily in the right order. I have to say, being able to dictate what I put in my books really helps me cope with the nonsense at school each day. And it takes my mind off any other worries or disappointments.'

'You mean like Rex not casting you as one of the Tudor queens for next autumn's drama production?'

I didn't know why Dinah felt compelled to humiliate everyone in the group. I remembered how hurt I was to have been turned down repeatedly for parts in Damian's plays, even non-speaking walk-on roles.

'Oh, Dinah, it's not as if Julia was the only one he turned down,' put in Karen. 'I mean, we'd all have liked to have been cast, and there weren't enough parts to go round. You can't blame Rex for Henry VIII only having six wives, can you?'

'Yes, but turning down a Tudor expert—'

Karen cut Dinah short by turning pointedly to me with an imploring look. I took the hint and introduced myself as I was the only one who hadn't done so, feeling as vulnerable as a newcomer at a meeting of Alcoholics Anonymous – not that I've ever been to one of those.

'I'm Sophie, and I'm May Sayers's great-niece. I don't know whether I met any of you when I used to stay with her in the summer holidays, when I was a child?' There were a couple of light nods from Louisa and Jessica. The others must have moved to the village recently, or else I'd made no impression upon them. 'Auntie May left me her cottage, and I've just come back to the UK after teaching abroad for the last four years.'

Julia perked up at the thought of another teacher in their midst. 'What subject?' she asked hopefully.

Her shoulders slumped when I said, 'English as a Foreign

Language', a common reaction from core subject teachers who tend to think of EFL teachers as also-rans. 'But I'm very keen on history,' I added, hoping not to have put her off me entirely. I needed to gather some allies in this group, in which clearly all was not sweetness and light (damn it, another 10p).

'So what do you write?' asked Dinah, who always seemed to cut to the chase (this meeting was becoming expensive).

'I've written all sorts of things over the years, mainly short stories and plays, but what I'd really like to write is a novel.' I didn't dare confess to abandoning five half-novels over the last four years, though I'd never ditched the manuscripts. Nor did I reveal Damian's rejection of my offer to write free plays to suit his cast. I tried to push that memory to the back of my mind, clinging on to thoughts of Auntie May for comfort and confidence.

'I'm thinking of writing a tribute to my aunt to provide a personal insight into the character behind the famous travelogues. It could be the preface to an anthology of her best essays.'

I was pleased with myself for coming up with that idea on the spur of the moment, even if it did mean another notional 10p.

'You mean a collection,' said Dinah curtly. 'An anthology means a set of works by multiple authors. A collection is by just one.'

She didn't say I was stupid, but she made me feel it.

I drained my glass of wine. 'So, can I interest anyone in another drink?' I needed one even if nobody else did. Everyone looked enthusiastic, and Bella wrote a list of their preferences and relieved me of a twenty pound note to place the order.

'That sounds a fascinating project,' said Karen kindly, patting my hand. 'What a lovely tribute to your aunt. I wish I'd had a famous writer as a relative.'

'It wouldn't help you get on if you did, though,' said Dinah. 'Only talent will do that.' Poor Karen looked hurt. Dinah seemed intent on quashing any pleasure that might be gained from the evening with her carefully sharpened barbs. Talk about the pen being mightier than the sword, Dinah was positively deadly.

I attempted to divert the conversation to give Karen time to recover. 'So tell me, Dinah, how do these meetings usually work?'

'We gather to share moral support, practical advice and best practice.'

Nul points for me, as far as I was concerned.

'Sometimes we bring our whips to share.'

'Whips?' I gasped, wondering whether I'd inadvertently hooked up with the wrong group.

Everyone else laughed before Julia clarified, 'Work In Progress. W. I. P.'

'And sometimes we share writing craft advice books or blog posts that we've found helpful,' put in Jacky. 'Or tips on how to self-publish, or how to submit your work to agents and publishers. Though only Karen has been properly published so far.'

I swivelled round to Karen, impressed likely.

'Well, if you count women's magazines,' she said with an apologetic smile.

Bella returned with my round of drinks, and all the group members raised their glasses to welcome me officially. I thought that was nice of them.

'So, why are you interested in joining our group?' asked Dinah. I hadn't expected the evening to turn into an interview. 'What can you bring to the table?'

Smirking, Bella tapped the Readathon collection box, and Dinah, scowling, dropped in 10p.

'For a start, I've just taken a job at Hector's House, so I'm your inroad to the book business.' I cringed at my awkward phrasing. 'In fact, on Hector's behalf, I'd like to invite you to hold your meetings there. A bookish environment might be more conducive to your art.'

Billy, helpful for once, emitted a loud belch at the bar as if to illustrate the unsuitability of our current surroundings.

'Also, as the new Assistant Entries Secretary for the Show Committee, I wanted to invite you to enter a float for the Village Show this year. We thought it might help you promote your work and your – our – organisation, raising awareness of the writers within the village.'

I sensed a release of tension around the table. You see, I come in peace, I thought. Then Dinah piped up.

'A float? That's all very well, but where are we supposed to find the actual float? And a vehicle to pull us? It's not as easy as you make it sound, you know.'

'Sorted.' I was glad to have the upper hand at last. 'I've already got the promise of a farm trailer for you, so it'll just be a case of decorating it. And I'm sure I can persuade Hector to tow it with his Land Rover.'

Julia, looking thoughtful, was a bit behind in the conversation. 'Yes, Hector's House would be much more appropriate. But of an evening? Do you think you could persuade him to open after hours for us? Some of us have day jobs, even though we aspire eventually to give them up and write full time.'

I sat back, on comfortable ground now. 'Oh, but I'm a key holder.' I offset my improvised white lie with an important truth. 'And I know how to work the coffee machine. I'm sure Hector would be fine with that.'

They all nodded approval.

'So you're a writer in residence at Hector's House?' queried Karen, looking impressed. Before I could disillusion her, Bella took the conversation in a new direction.

'But what shall we do for the float? What theme should we take?'

'How about our writing heroes?' suggested Jacky. 'It might be a bit obvious, but it would certainly be fun. Bags I Charles Dickens!'

'That gives you less than eight weeks to grow a beard. But I'm sure you could do it if you put your mind to it.'

Jacky ignored Dinah.

'Ooh, Barbara Cartland for me!' said Karen. 'I've got lots of pink things.'

'Just come as you are,' murmured Dinah.

For the rest of the evening, we planned who we'd be and what we'd wear. Each member quickly nominated a favourite author. Even Dinah started to enter into the spirit of it. Anxious to impress, I claimed Virginia Woolf. When I left, I realised that I was already an accepted member of the group. That felt good.

Only later, lying in bed, did I realise I'd missed a trick: I should have gone as my great aunt. At least then, I'd have felt safer. Auntie May had so many friends in the village – surely no-one would hurt her?

Or had they already done so?

13

THE LEADING MAN

'What surprised me most was that there wasn't a single man among them,' I told Hector next morning, as I dried the cups and saucers after the morning rush.

Hector looked up from his computer keyboard. 'You mean there wasn't a man who was unmarried, or there wasn't a man at all?'

'The latter. I mean, you'd think statistically speaking, somewhere in a village of this size, there'd be a man interested in writing a book, wouldn't you?'

I continued wiping the tearoom tables with a dishcloth. Hector shrugged.

'Maybe not at this time of year. All too busy nurturing their dahlias.'

'Is that a euphemism?' At least I made him laugh.

'For the Village Show. Sprucing up their gardens, ready to submit some winning entries.'

'But now they can win something by writing, thanks to the new May Sayers Nature Writing Cup.'

Hector got up from his stool and came out from behind the counter to stroll around the shop, stretching his long, lean legs. He'd been sitting much longer than was healthy.

'We'll see. It takes a while to get new ideas off the ground round here, but they catch on in the end. So, are you now an official member of their merry throng, or was that a one-off visit? Did they leave you inspired? Did you rattle off a sonnet in their praise as soon as you got home?'

I wondered whether he was making a gentle dig at my literary aspirations.

'Yes, I've joined, but no to the sonnet. But I did persuade them that the more natural home for their meetings might be here, rather than The Bluebird.'

Hector brightened. 'Really? Well done, Sophie. Good work.'

'Provided you agree to pull their float on Show Day,' I added quickly, before I lost my nerve. 'You'll need to supply me with a key to the shop so I can open up for them after hours. Unless of course you want to join the Wendlebury Writers too? You could be our token man.'

He stopped where he stood by the self-help section and fixed me with a suspicious look.

'Oh, come on, it'll be worth your while. They're bound to buy books if they're meeting here regularly. And stationery. Not to mention the tea and cake.'

He spent a moment rearranging the gardening books that lay flat, face up, on the table at the centre of the room.

'If it's single men you're after, try the parish magazine.'

I frowned. Had he not listened to what I'd been saying?

'You'll find the opportunity for a night out at a different club or organisation every day of the week. Chess club, history association, drama club. There may not be any single men at the drama club just now, but that doesn't seem to stop Rex from playing the field.' He leaned into the window to pick up a book that had somehow fallen forward off its display stand. 'So there's never any shortage of drama.'

'Really? What goes on there, then?'

'I'd class it as opera rather than drama. Soap opera, that is. Closest thing the village has got to a wife-swapping club. The numbers are a bit uneven – only a couple of men against a horde of women, and both of them are spoken for. Ian's married and Rex lives with the lovely Dido.'

'Aren't there any single men who might want to go along? Sounds like exactly the right club for any men who are looking for girlfriends.'

'That would be fine if there were any. But the only single men living in this village are still at school, or too old to be of romantic interest to anyone, like Billy. Classic Cotswold village problem. The youngsters can't afford to live here after they leave school. They go off to university and don't come back. As I did myself, at least for a while.'

The doorbell jangled, and Joshua crossed the threshold and raised his tweed cap to me. 'Present company excepted,' added Hector, and I had to suppress a giggle.

I returned to my station at the tearoom counter and gave Joshua a dutiful welcome. His disproportionately appreciative smile made me realise how much of his day he must spend alone.

'Good morning, my dear. And Hector.' Joshua nodded to acknowledge my boss, now back behind the shop counter putting on some Mozart. 'Just thought I'd take a stroll up here to put my young friend's waitressing skills to the test.'

Hector sat back and looked at him with a friendly expression. 'Yes, thanks, Joshua. She's the dabbest hand with a dishcloth that a bookseller could wish for.'

I wondered whether they were in league together.

Joshua was clearly one of the customers who only came here for the company, not even glancing at the bookshelves. He gave a small smile.

'I'm glad to see Sophie making herself at home here in Wendlebury. She's joined the Wendlebury Writers now too.' Goodness knows who had told him that. Probably Carol at the Village Shop. Or he'd had me followed.

'After a fashion,' said Hector. 'Though not without roping me in to tow their Show float.'

'Quite right too,' said Joshua. 'You pull your weight, young man. Though the assembled throng will require more than your weight, I'll wager.'

Joshua and Hector both chortled.

'We've just been talking about whether I should join the Wendlebury Players.' I didn't understand why they exchanged glances. 'So what sort of plays do they do?'

'Anything with a large cast of women at the moment,' said Hector. 'Either that or the women play men's parts. A bit like doing Shakespeare in a single-sex high school, only without the looks or talent.'

Joshua tutted. 'Now, now, Hector, they're not as bad as all that.'

'But you saw their *Sound of Music*? Linda Absolom really was too old to play Maria, and as for Rex shrinking the family to three outsized teenaged girls, aged forty plus, that stretched our willing suspension of disbelief beyond breaking point. But at least everyone in the audience knew the words so they could sing along when the cast forgot them, whether or not Rex wanted them to. I have to admit, though, Joshua, their shows haven't been the same since you left the group.'

Joshua tottered over to the tearoom area. 'A black coffee please, my dear.' He lowered himself onto one of the chairs, resting both hands on his walking stick in front of him to keep his balance. I dropped a capsule into the coffee machine, pressed the water button, and set the full cup on the table in front of him.

'My drama days are over now, Hector. Let the youngsters take their turn.' He splashed enough milk from the Joy Adamson's *Born Free* jug to turn the coffee opaque. 'And I certainly couldn't cope with the ladies who are members there now. I don't hold with the games Rex plays. Once you've found one good woman, why go elsewhere, even if she does stop up in the City during the week?'

'Dido, you mean? Yes, I've never understood what she sees in him – a successful businesswoman like that settling for a failed conjuror.' Hector shrugged. 'But who knows? Maybe she's got a fancy man up in London for weekdays, and Rex is her comic relief for weekends. Or maybe when he learned his conjuring skills, he picked up a bit of hypnosis too, and he's now got her in a permanent trance of obedience. He clicks his fingers and she does what he likes.'

I hadn't yet met Dido, but I would certainly keep a lookout for her now. What kind of woman could she be? Both men looked thoughtful for a moment, lost in their separate reveries of what it might be like to have hypnotic powers.

Then I had a brainwave. Maybe Hector was right: I was a woman of ideas.

'It sounds like what they need is a play written specially to suit their membership. One with lots of women in it. I could have a go at that. I used to write scripts for my boyfriend's drama company.' I worried for a moment that I was over-reaching myself. 'Or at least, I could ask my new friends at the Wendlebury Writers to collaborate.'

'I'd be impressed if you managed that. There's no love lost

between the Wendlebury Writers and Rex, not after that fiasco last year when he fired three of them from the cast halfway through the production of *Daisy Pulls It Off*. Dinah, Jacky and Karen, wasn't it?'

'Why would he do that?' I asked, astonished that they'd still wanted to audition for his next play after such humiliation.

'Refused his advances, I suspect,' said Hector. 'Or maybe because they're Dido's friends and he didn't want them telling tales on his antics. Not that he cares. There always seem to be women ready to rush into the void, where Rex is concerned. Or so he thinks. I'm not sure the women he chases after see it that way. If I were a woman, he'd strike me as slimy. And his constant habit of showing off his conjuring tricks would really pall after the first date.'

'Depends what sort of tricks they are,' I said. 'He'd never have an excuse for not giving his date flowers.'

'Still, it's about time he put all that behind him. It's got to be twenty years since he last worked as a professional magician. He's just a drama teacher now.'

I'd never heard Hector talk so uncharitably about anyone and wondered what cause he had for such personal bitterness. Surely he hadn't made a romantic bid for Rex himself, the inevitable rejection leaving him with a grudge?

'I'd like to meet this Rex,' I said thoughtfully. 'Only to see what he's like. He sounds extraordinary.'

'Don't let yourself be taken in by him.' Joshua sounded genuinely concerned.

'Don't worry about that. I'm immune. My last boyfriend, Damian, was an actor.'

Hector raised his eyebrows. 'Ex-boyfriend?'

I nodded. "Fraid so. I left him behind in Frankfurt to grow up.

He didn't want to settle down, and I got fed up waiting for him to get his act together, so to speak.'

Hector returned to his computer and started tapping away at the keyboard. 'Been together long?' I got the impression he wasn't really listening to my answer.

'Too long. Too long for someone who wasn't prepared to make a commitment, that is. God knows where he is now – off on tour again somewhere, I expect. He runs a travelling English language theatre company which targets expats' hot spots in Europe. That's all very well when you're fresh out of uni, but hardly a lifelong career prospect.'

I chose my words carefully so as to seem less gullible than I now felt. 'I thought it was going to be fun to start with. We thought we'd come up with the Big Idea, the perfect alternative to what Damian called the Golden Handcuffs of the Milk Round – you know, when big businesses come to universities to offer undergraduates fantastic corporate jobs. The sort that have you married and mortgaged in minutes, sentencing you to a life of nine-till-five slog to pay it off before you retire.'

I made myself a cappuccino to steel my nerves.

'Instead, I was tied down for only a few weeks to an intensive English language teaching course, which Damian said would be my passport to freedom. He said I'd be able to work anywhere he took his travelling theatre company. He set it up and recruited a few other drama graduates to join him, but their VW camper van had his stage name on it: Damian Drammaticas. His real surname is Jones. They planned to tour Europe, performing with modern minimalist staging, to save money, to expat audiences and foreigners keen on improving their English.'

Joshua nodded approval. I might have known that as a fellow actor he would take Damian's side.

'Our businesses would cross-fertilise. I was to spread word of their performances to my clientele and pay to advertise my services in their programme.'

'Smart move,' put in Hector, paying attention again now that we were discussing enterprise.

'Ha, that's easy for you to say. But what started out as a smart idea left me feeling like I was on the wrong end of a see-saw. I was left permanently in the air, with Damian and the rest of the cast all sitting on the other end. They spent increasing amounts of time away from where I was working, only returning to sleep on my floor between gigs and freeload from my fridge. They basked at French seaside resorts, while I slaved in Paris, even through August.'

Hector looked dubious. 'And you don't miss living abroad? You're not sorry you moved to Wendlebury? You're not tempted to go back if you get bored here?'

I frowned. 'No. I may not be a natural nomad like my aunt, but I had the good sense to move on when the time was right.'

'And the good sense to have an aunt die and leave you a house to live in,' he murmured, too quietly for Joshua to hear. Then he had the decency to look abashed for being so insensitive. 'I'm sorry. I know it wasn't really like that. Did she leave you the royalties too? If so, you might not even need to work for a living. Her royalties must be quite decent, the amount of books she sells. And, though I hate to say it, her sales will probably rise, at least for a little while, following her death. Copyright lasts seventy years after an author's death.'

I glanced at Joshua, wondering whether he'd somehow persuaded her to leave them to him.

'Seventy years, eh? That would see me out.' Joshua sounded thoughtful. Surely he hadn't bumped her off for her royalties without even knowing how long they lasted?

I shrugged. 'I've no idea. My dad's been dealing with her

probate. I don't really know how royalties work or whether they'd amount to much. I'm just grateful she left me the cottage.'

I returned to work without further remark, washing up Joshua's cup as he headed out of the door, laying the tables ready for the next customers, and wondering why Dad hadn't told me about the royalties. It seemed awfully odd to me.

14

TAKING STOCK

I was ready for the day off on Sunday. I needed to find the local supermarket and stock the larder up with a little more variety than the bread, honey, tinned soup and local fresh eggs that had been my staple diet all week. I also had to plan my new pupils' first lessons. I had three children booked in for English coaching, one each afternoon on the Tuesday, Wednesday and Thursday, for half an hour soon after the end of the school day.

Hector had given me a couple of helpful brochures of academic books for primary school age children. Poring over these brochures at Auntie May's desk, I realised how little I knew about the current English school curriculum. Before going any further, I thought it best to set up a meeting with someone from the village school to make sure that the support I provided was appropriate, and that offering private lessons would not affect relations between the bookshop and the school. I didn't want it to seem as if I was accusing the school of inadequate teaching.

I decided to call in at the school the next day to make an appointment to visit their headmaster or headmistress. This excused me from any further preparation in the meantime, other than rereading the brochures Hector had given me.

I appreciated Hector's thoughtfulness. He could easily have told me to teach in my own time at home, rather than in the shop, and I wouldn't have blamed him. Damian had never been this helpful, going out of his way to make a noise when I'd had private pupils back to my flat, or leaving coffee cups on the small desk where I did my teaching. I'd tell myself he was just being a forgetful theatrical type, but now Hector's example showed Damian in a less flattering light.

To help prepare my visit to the school, I looked up its website. The school seemed pleasant enough, though very different to the luxurious international schools I'd been used to working in. These were all privately owned and run, funded by vast fees from the globetrotting businesspeople whose children attended them. Modern, spacious and comfortable facilities were the least standards expected by parents used to staying in five-star hotels and flying first-class.

Wendlebury Barrow Primary School was, by contrast, housed in a shabby Victorian building. Attached was the cottage formerly occupied by the head teacher in the days when a single member of staff would have been all it employed, regardless of the number of pupils. Headmistresses would have been single, because, as the website informed me, female teachers were required to give up their posts on marriage. Now the school was run by a headmaster, plus four teachers, for around a hundred pupils. Despite the tumbledown building, the children looked happy and shining with health in their neat little blue and grey uniforms.

For a moment, I felt guilty for having to myself a cottage that would have once housed a family. Auntie May had been born and raised there, along with her three siblings, by her parents, with the two bedrooms between the lot of them. And there was me having thought the cottage, with its low ceilings and narrow doorways, was a bit on the small side.

I spent the rest of the day pottering about the house, unpacking the rest of my possessions, and allowing them to be absorbed among hers. I thought that should make the house feel a little more like my own. But sitting down at Auntie May's writing desk that evening, I felt like some kind of ghost in reverse, haunting with my presence where Auntie May really belonged. I felt like an imposter, not least when I opened the notebook containing my latest piece of writing: a few lines about my break-up with Damian.

With the critical eye that comes only when you've set a piece of work aside for a few weeks, I picked up a red biro from the carved sandalwood pencil pot on top of the desk, slashing through superfluous words and awkward phrases until the page looked like the scene of a massacre. I sat back and sighed. Maybe I was trying to write the wrong thing.

I looked on top of the desk for inspiration. Considering how many souvenirs from May's travels were dotted about other parts of the house, I thought it seemed surprisingly empty with just the pencil pot and the telephone. I decided to personalise it with some photos and went upstairs to fetch some from the only bag I hadn't yet unpacked.

I'd stowed it under Auntie May's high brass bedstead, so I pulled it out and heaved it on top. In an old jiffy bag was my small store of photos, including one picture of me and May when I was about five, another with my parents at my graduation, and a selfie of me with Damian beneath the Eiffel Tower. We'd taken this picture on his return from his trip to the French coast without me. I'd never noticed till now how strained both our smiles looked.

Suddenly it struck me how hugely supportive I'd been to have tagged along with Damian so blindly. It's not as if the other members of his drama group were welcoming. They used me only to do the jobs they didn't want to do, like selling programmes and taking tickets. You'd have thought I was some sort of intern rather than the person subsidising them.

I climbed onto May's bed and sat back against the big soft pillows, staring at the photo for a bit, trying to see Damian with the admiration and love that I'd felt before. After lying there for a little while, I removed the photo from its frame, put it in the jiffy bag, returned the jiffy bag to the suitcase, and stowed it back under the bed. Then I went downstairs to put the other framed photos on the desk, as well as the now empty frame.

I'd come to a critical decision: I was now recruiting for a replacement for Damian. But where on earth would I find one in a village populated only by families, the elderly, mad men and murderers?

15

TEACHING THE TEACHERS

At 8.50 the following morning, I detoured to the village school to introduce myself to its secretary, almost getting mown down in the rush of small children, scooters and dogs on leads racing to arrive before the school bell rang. The current staff had clearly tried to make the squat, dark building look as welcoming as possible within the constraints of its heritage status. The spooky Gothic windows were redeemed by cheerful pieces of children's handicraft on deep windowsills: wobbly clay pots and papier-mâché animals, each as different as the children now swarming around me on their way to the playground.

I didn't need to ask directions to the office, as someone had helpfully painted bright orange footprints from the school gate. These led to a bottle green wooden door at the centre of the building between two arched entrances marked 'Boys' and 'Girls'. I wanted to mark this one 'Don't Know'.

I found myself in a dark narrow passage with identical doors either side, one marked 'Office' and the other 'Head'. It reminded me of the corridor that Alice finds when she falls down the rabbit-hole. I half expected to find a table in the hall bearing a bottle labelled 'Drink Me'.

The Office door was already open. Beyond were two mums waiting their turn to speak to a competent-looking secretary fielding a phone call behind an old oak desk. She looked about my age, her long dark hair was tied back in a neat ponytail, and she wore a practical slate-coloured linen shift.

'No, it's definitely forty-eight hours after the last episode of vomiting before Timmy can come back to school, Mrs Evans, even if you do have a hairdresser's appointment this morning. I'm sorry, but that's the rule.'

The two mums were exchanging knowing looks.

'Quite right too!' said one. I waited patiently while she handed in an outgrown school uniform for the spare clothes box and the other raided the Lost Property box, grumbling.

'What I don't understand is why he didn't notice he'd come home in only one shoe.'

She found the missing shoe, and also pulled out three other items labelled with her son's name. They each smiled at me as they left the office, their missions accomplished.

'Ooh, hello, Miss Sayers, we've heard about you,' said the shoeless boy's mum. I hoped it had all been good.

The secretary greeted me in a friendly manner before excusing herself to brush past me into the hall. I watched through the open door as she hauled on the bell-rope to signal to the children that the school day was about to begin. It struck me as dangerous to have a rope like that hanging within easy reach of young children.

Through the other window I watched dozens of pupils line up in the playground. Several latecomers hurtled past, book bags flying behind them. Then the secretary returned to her desk, and I waited a moment while we both savoured the subsequent calm.

She picked up a bunch of lavender that had been left in her in-tray by an anonymous benefactor, stems wrapped neatly in tin foil, held the posy up to her face and breathed in its heady scent.

'Mmm, the perfect aromatherapy treatment for a busy school office.' She smiled at me. 'Now, what can I do for you this morning? You're new to the village, aren't you? I don't suppose you've brought a bevy of primary-school-age children to enrol here?'

'Sorry, can't help on that one.'

'Pity. Our numbers will be falling at the beginning of next term. The joining class is five fewer than the leavers' class. I've got to the point now where I assess every newcomer for their fecundity, hoping they've got a huge brood of under-elevens.' She sighed. 'The window-cleaner gave me a funny look after I asked him about his family plans the other day. I hope he didn't think I fancied him.'

I laughed. She didn't seem like my idea of the average school secretary. 'I'm Sophie Sayers, by the way. Very much single and childless at the moment, but never say die. I may only have just moved to the village, but I might end up staying and having dozens of children eventually. Can't promise any in time for this September, though.'

She held out her hand to shake mine. 'Ella Berry. School Business Manager. Welcome to the village. Hmm, Sophie Sayers. Would you be related to May Sayers, by any chance?'

I nodded.

'Thought so. We loved May. She used to come in to speak to the children about her travels and her books. She could rustle up a handy talk for any topic. Africa, India, America. There weren't many places she hadn't been, and she always brought plenty of show-and-tell items to illustrate talks. She was invaluable for World Book Day, sharing her love of books with the children and encouraging them to read and write. Are you also a writer? Have you inherited her writing talent? Or her itchy feet?'

'The itchy feet, certainly. I've spent the whole of my career so far teaching English around Europe. And I do love books, and reading and writing. I've yet to publish anything myself, I'm hoping to eventually.'

'Oh good, let us know where you've lived and we'll rope you in when we're doing topics about European countries. With so few staff, we're always on the scrounge for volunteers' time. Is that what you're here for today? Come to join our team of volunteers that hears children reading?'

For a moment I felt wrong-footed. Instead of seizing the opportunity to empty parents' pockets, should I just be offering my services free of charge to the community?

At that point an immaculately tailored woman who had presumably become a mother relatively late in life appeared in the doorway, a crocodile-skin purse in one hand.

'I am in receipt of your text message about Felicity's dinner money,' she said, opening her purse and elbowing me aside in one slick movement. 'I assume you have change?'

'That's £23.50, please, Mrs Absolom,' said Ella, consulting a spreadsheet on her computer screen.

Mrs Absolom scrabbled in her purse. 'I hope you have change of a fifty.'

Ella opened a drawer and pulled out an old-fashioned cash box marked 'Dinner Money'. She counted out the change in one pound and fifty pence coins.

Mrs Absolom looked disdainful. 'I don't know what I'm supposed to do with those.'

Her dismissive attitude to so much money gave me hope that at least some village families might be wealthy enough to pay my coaching fees. Then she pointed imperiously to the lavender.

'And you shouldn't have dreadful stinking flowers like that in school. So bad for hay fever. Just attracts pests.' Without waiting for a reply, she stalked out, coughing pointedly.

Ella grinned as Mrs Absolom slammed the front door behind her. 'Hmm, I guess that means Mrs Absolom isn't my secret admirer. I reckon some Year 6 boy picked them from the school garden and wrapped them in foil from his packed lunch. A few of them have got a bit of a crush on me just now. Goodness, those boys are more than ready to move up to Big School. They need to meet girls closer to their own age.'

She peeled off the foil, revealing tell-tale scraps of cheese and tomato among the lavender stems. She picked them off patiently and dropped them in the bin. 'Still, peace at last! Now, what can I do for you?'

I explained my new coaching practice to Ella and enquired whether the school might be happy to make referrals. She couldn't have been more supportive.

'So, you're working for the lovely Hector, eh?' I couldn't stop myself flashing a glance at her left hand to check whether she was single. 'Your coaching sounds a great idea, and the bookshop is a perfect setting for paid lessons. You'll be ideal for those that need more individual attention and time than we can offer within the school day. The Head will be happy for you to chat with our teacher in charge of literacy for a steer on the curriculum. Let me know when you want to make an appointment. In the meantime, I can give you the crib sheets we've distributed to parents with tips on how to help their children with reading and writing. You'll have to get government certification to confirm that you're safe to work with children, but I can give you the application form for that. I don't know whether you had it before you moved abroad, but even if you did, you'll need to reapply, because the rules change every five minutes.'

She turned to open the low filing cabinet behind her, instantly finding the right pocket and pulling out a neatly formatted double-sided sheet of paper to give me.

'And if, in return, you'd like to spend any time volunteering to help us revamp the school library, I'm sure you'll be especially welcome.'

She gave me her business card. Not for nothing was she School Business Manager rather than secretary, I realised. I scribbled down my own contact details on a scrap of paper and invited her to join me in the tearoom for a coffee any time she fancied one. She seemed the first truly sensible, straightforward, ordinary person that I'd met since I'd arrived in the village. That was suspicious in itself. There had to be a catch.

16

LESSON TIME

I headed back down the High Street to Hector's House.

'I've just been up to the school,' I announced. 'That Ella Berry, the School Business Manager, seems nice. She's asked me to go and do what my auntie May did at school.'

Hector, already installed behind the counter and tapping away at his laptop as I came through the door, looked up and stopped typing for a moment.

'If you're going to be their writer-in-residence, doesn't it require that you actually write something first?'

I groaned. 'Is that what she was? I thought she just went in to talk to the children now and again.' I realised it was confession time. 'The thing is, I've written loads, but I've never shared it with anyone before, apart from Damian, my ex. I'm still at the polishing stage.' To be honest, I was more at the writing-and-screwing-up-and-throwing-in-the-bin stage. 'And anyway, if I'm in there helping with their library as a volunteer, it's pretty certain that when they need more books, they'll order through your shop.'

'They do that already anyway,' said Hector.

I set my bag down behind the counter in time to turn the coffee maker on before the morning mums came in.

* * *

With no customers spoiling our peace and quiet after the morning rush, Hector carried on bashing away at his keyboard. I couldn't believe how long he spent fussing over his accounts. I hadn't appreciated before how much administrative work went into running a bookshop – I'd assumed that bookshops, like libraries, were oases of calm and order. But it appeared that behind the scenes there was frantic activity keeping the place afloat.

'Can't I help you with that, Hector?' I asked, sure so much screen time couldn't be good for his eyesight, or his mental health.

'What? No, no, don't worry, only I can do this.' He didn't even look up. 'But you could help by making me another latte. Need to perk the old brain up here.'

Until then I'd assumed Hector was totally on top of the bread-and-butter side of the business, which I was slowly starting to understand: identifying the best books to stock, ordering them in, shelving them, then returning for credit the ones that did nothing but gather dust. I had never thought of there being a sell-by date on books before, but any that weren't sold within a reasonable time-frame were jettisoned to make room for replacements that might make more money. Publishers' sales reps did their best during regular visits to convince us that their books would boost our profits, but I often caught Hector tutting and shaking his head as he inputted data to the computer at the bookshop counter.

'Worried about your books?' I asked sympathetically, setting down his latte on his mouse mat. 'I mean, accounts, not books. If you are, I think you could make more use of me than you do.'

He looked up with a quizzical expression. 'I'm happy with what you're doing, thank you. The tearoom's thriving and making a bigger contribution to the bottom line than before. That idea of yours to sell birthday cakes was brilliant. I never knew there were so many people in the village who had birthdays.' As usual, I wasn't sure whether he was joking. 'You're doing good work with the window displays too.'

He turned back to his computer and carried on typing.

* * *

The arrival of the first after-school mums as their children crashed through the door made Hector finally move from his stool mid-afternoon. As always, there was plenty of browsing, but not a lot of buying. Books were popular purchases for children's birthday presents, as were book tokens, which came back into the shop after their parties with the reliability of a homing pigeon. Sometimes book tokens with blatant children's designs were deployed by mums to buy adult fiction or cookbooks or gardening books, or presents to post to other relatives. I hoped they'd bought them off their children rather than just purloining them, though it seemed a shame the children didn't want to use them. It was always a joy to see a little boy or girl choose a new favourite book with a birthday token.

Currently travel books were most popular among the mums. My new shop window display on a summer holiday theme attracted a bit of chatter about their plans for the break from school.

'We're off to Turkey,' said one, 'but we won't be leaving the resort. They've got everything there we need – kids' club, swimming pool, health club. We don't need a guide to the country, unless it's got a map to the resort bar.'

I swear I heard my auntie May turn in her grave.

The first of my new pupils appeared just after I'd finished clearing away following the post-school tea trade: a small blonde girl named Jemima, in Year 2, aged seven, clutching her book bag. Her mum ushered her across the threshold and made a brusque introduction.

'I can't get her to read for her fifteen minutes every day,' she said, thrusting a £10 note into my hand. 'So I'm delegating it to you.'

'But we've only got half an hour, so that's only two days' worth of reading homework.'

The woman shrugged. 'That's what I'm paying you for. Motivational skills. She won't listen to her mother. I thought you might make her want to read.' And with that she departed, leaving Hector shaking his head in admonition at the mother rather than the child.

Jemima looked up at me, wide-eyed. I couldn't decide whether this was in fear or indignation. I took her by the hand and led her to one of the tearoom tables where we sat down together. She looked at me levelly.

'So what's the problem, Jemima?'

The little girl emptied the contents of her book bag onto the table. 'Have you seen our school reading books?' She opened a large white book with a dated line drawing on the cover, called *Tommy and Tammy Tidy their Bedrooms*, riffling through the pages. The typeface dated it to the 1980s, but the domestic setting for the tale of the two unprepossessing children looked barely post-war. I guessed the storyline was wish-fulfilment, written by a weary parent-turned-author.

'Goodness, are you reading that as a punishment?'

'Sort of,' replied Jemima. 'Once we've got through this series, we're free readers and then we can read whatever we like. We're meant to read one of these books every night, but I can't be doing with it.'

She had clearly inherited her mother's defeatism.

I flicked through the book again. 'But can you read it? Or are the words too hard?'

'No, they're easy-peasy. They're just too boring.'

I closed the book and leaned forward, ready to negotiate. 'Look, I'll make a deal with you. For every night you spend fifteen minutes reading your school book, I'll give you a star sticker.' I'd found some of these in my work bag when I was unpacking and had the foresight to bring them into the shop for my new pupils. 'Then, when you've got a card full of stars, you can choose a new book from the shop as a reward. It can be any book you positively want to read, not a reading scheme one. When you're in Hector's House, you *are* a free reader, so long as you read your school books too. How's that sound?'

I took her by the hand and led her over to the children's section, and encouraged her to pick up and dip into whichever books took her fancy.

'I want that one,' she asserted after a minute, grabbing with both hands a pink sparkly book about fairies with dense, challenging text on every page. 'Will you save it for me please so no-one else gets it?'

She stroked the cover proprietorially. I nodded. 'I'm sure it can be arranged. Mr Munro will put your name on it and keep it behind the counter for you. So let's now read your school book, and if you read it nicely for me, you can read one page of the fairy book at the end as a reward. Then every day on your way home from school, come in and tell me about the school book you've read the night before, and we'll put another star on your card. How's that sound?'

She nodded and held out her hand for me to shake. 'Deal.' I wondered what kind of wheeler-dealing went on in the village school playground to make a seven-year-old such an astute businesswoman. 'Would you like me to make you a friendship bracelet? What's your favourite colour? I gave your auntie a purple rubber band one last year after she picked me up when I fell over in the park, but we don't like those any more. We like making bracelets out of string now. I'm going to be a fairy in the Village Show this year. So this book will be good for giving me fashion tips. What will you be?' She didn't pause long enough for me to answer, keen to pursue her own agenda. 'Please don't be another fairy. I can't be doing with the competition.'

When her half hour was up, Jemima skipped happily out of the door with her mum. Only then did I realise that Hector had been watching the whole process with considerable approval. He gave me a playful smile.

'So, not another fairy, then. What are you dressing up as?'

'The Wendlebury Writers are all going as their writing heroes, and I said I'd be Virginia Woolf. Though to be honest, I'm wondering whether I should have said I'd go as my aunt.'

'Just as well if you don't. Otherwise you'll confuse any old dears who have forgotten she's dead and they'll all be thinking you're her.'

He came over to sit opposite me at the tearoom table and reached across to turn my head to one side, so he could see my profile. I jumped slightly as he touched me, his forefinger under my chin. It felt embarrassingly intimate. After all, he was my boss.

'Virginia Woolf,' he declared. 'You've got the right nose for her, but the wrong colour eyes. Hers were grey. Yours are blue – forget-me-not blue.'

He gazed at me critically, as if trying to picture the transformation. Perhaps he fancied himself as a personal stylist.

Realising I was blushing, I reeled off the list of the authors the other writers had chosen, but I couldn't get his mind off Virginia Woolf. He went over to the classics section and pulled out a slim paperback.

'Here you go.' He held up a copy of *A Room of One's Own*, the back cover of which featured a wistful black and white profile photo of the author as a young woman. 'Easy-peasy, as your young friend would say. You won't even need to bother with make-up. Leave that to Barbara Cartland.'

He reached above the door to set the shop's burglar alarm for the night. I knew we'd have to leave within five minutes or it would go off, but I didn't want to cut our conversation short.

'You couldn't choose a finer role model for your writing either,' he continued, apparently unhurried. 'She had a high-achieving ancestor too, in her father, Leslie Stephen.' He picked a portrait from the rack of greetings cards. 'Here's what's probably the most famous photo of her. She had a beautiful profile.'

I thought her hair looked a bit untidy.

'Take it home and you can use it to get the hairstyle right. Then maybe later we can get a photo of you posing as Virginia in the shop and put it on our website and social media. The local paper might like to do a story on it for a bit of publicity for the shop when they're having a slow news week during the summer. It would be good for your writing career too, of course.'

He fixed me with a serious gaze, as if daring me to confess that I was nowhere near close to publishing anything.

'And good for the other Wendlebury Writers too,' I suggested, anxious to broaden his focus, while secretly adding 'Hector's House writer-in-residence' to my list of authorly ambitions.

We left the building together. As I headed homeward up the High Street, I considered that I never once had writer's block when it came to lists. Trying to write anything longer than a list was where the trouble started. I was worried that another of Damian's predictions might come true: that nothing would ever happen here to inspire me to write more. That concerned me even more than my fear of being murdered in my bed.

17

IN WOOLF'S CLOTHING

As soon as I got home, I had another rummage through Auntie May's big old-fashioned oak wardrobe for a suitable dress for Virginia Woolf. As I opened the wardrobe's double doors, the familiar smell of her exotic Eastern perfumes wafted out to greet me. I almost expected to find her hiding at the back there, as if in some latter-day Narnia.

I ran my hands back and forth through her flowing dresses, savouring the feel of the smooth fabric against my skin. Auntie May had always favoured long dresses at home, presumably compensating for the many months she spent abroad each year in more practical travelling clothes: khaki cargo trousers, vest tops and cool cotton shift dresses. These were shelved at the top of the wardrobe, as she never wore them around the village.

I pulled down a sage green safari suit and held the jacket up against me, trying to cast myself in her role of seasoned traveller. For a moment I considered posing as Ernest Hemingway, with an elephant gun under one arm, but I didn't want to disappoint Hector's Virginia Woolf fantasy, or be mistaken for a supporter of the local hunt.

I stowed the suit away and pulled out a few dresses, flinging them on the bed for further consideration. An ankle-length silk dress with a fringed hem jumped out as being particularly suitable. Made in a loose low-waisted cut, presumably to guard against the heat in its country of origin (India, perhaps?), it could easily pass for 1930s-style.

I picked up my smartphone to do a quick Google, making sure I'd got Virginia's dates right. With that minor point confirmed, I slipped off the jeans and t-shirt I'd worn to the shop and pulled the dress over my head. It slid down as easily as a dropped theatre curtain, coming to rest in exactly the right places. Closing the heavy door of the wardrobe, I gazed at myself in the mirror. It was certainly a dress in which I'd be happy to be seen in public. The cool caress of the slippery silk against my bare skin hit the spot on this warm evening.

I decided to keep it on to get into my part. Scraping my hair back into a ponytail, I doubled it over in a vague approximation of a low bun at the nape of my neck. Then I grabbed Hector's copy of *A Room of One's Own* and headed for the garden, pausing only to pour a glass of chilled white wine from the fridge on the way out. I wasn't sure whether Virginia Woolf went much on Chardonnay, but I didn't think she'd object.

* * *

A little later, I woke up with a shiver when a gentle puff of wind passed across my face, unexpected on such a still, humid evening. There was Joshua, sitting in the garden chair next to mine, leaning forward, both hands on his stick. I suspected he'd blown on me to wake me up gently. At least, I hoped it was a blow and not a sneeze. In his hand was a parcel addressed to me that he'd taken in from the postman while I was at work.

'Good afternoon, Miss Sayers.' He held out the parcel. I immediately recognised Damian's handwriting on the address label. 'If I'm not much mistaken, that's one of May's old frocks, is it not?' He ran his eyes appreciatively down my body. 'Yes, I remember seeing May in that dress the first time she brought it back from Hyderabad.'

Unsure whether he was thinking of my body or May's beneath the cheesecloth, I shivered again, despite the heat.

I sat up, set the wineglass and book on the ground, and pulled the dress down over my legs. It had slipped up to thigh level while I'd had my feet on the table. 'It's my costume for the Village Show: Virginia Woolf. I'm trying it out. Do you think this looks right for the 1930s?'

He gave me an old-fashioned look. 'My dear, you look the image of May's mother, who would have been Miss Woolf's contemporary.'

So now I was May's mother. This family resemblance was getting beyond a joke. I was starting to want to be my own person.

To distract myself from that disturbing thought, I chattered on for a bit, telling him who the others in the Wendlebury Writers had chosen as their Literary Heroes. Then, having thanked him for taking in the parcel for me, I made an excuse to go back indoors, saying I didn't have much time to spare before the Wendlebury Players' meeting. Which was true, but really I couldn't bear not to open Damian's parcel. I wondered whether he was feeling contrite and wanted to make up.

Contrite? Unlikely. Vengeful? Perhaps. After all, it was his idea that I should be murdered in Wendlebury Barrow.

I gave the parcel a quick shake to check whether it was ticking. Then, in the kitchen with the vegetable knife, I cut through the Sellotape more quickly than I should have done, nicking my left thumb in the process. Ripping off the brown paper, I found inside neither a bomb nor a gift, but a bundle of post that had come to my old flat, of which Damian and his theatrical friends had taken over the tenancy. The bundle consisted entirely of circulars and rubbish that I didn't want. The only personal touch was a dog-eared postcard of a familiar view of the Rhine, which I remembered buying months before I'd left Frankfurt and never sending to anyone. I flipped it over, thinking Damian might have written a message to me, but it was blank. If it hadn't been for the handwriting on the address label, the parcel might as well have been sent by the landlord.

With a sigh, I headed for the front room, flung the circulars on the copper-topped Moroccan coffee table, and sank onto the sofa, curling up and hugging my knees to my chest for comfort. Although it was a warm evening, I felt the need for a hug, but no-one was about to give me one.

Then something caught my eye in the brass wire cage on the front door that held the post as it came through the letterbox. There in the basket was another postcard, the picture facing me. I could tell it was from Germany, being as it showed a classic town square edged with half-timbered houses. Damian! I'd underestimated him. No wonder he hadn't included a note in the parcel – he'd sent the postcard separately to give me the fun of getting two pieces of post. I should have credited him with being more thoughtful. He was probably anxious for my welfare, given his warnings about the dangers of village life.

I leapt up from the sofa and grabbed the postcard from the cage, turning it over eagerly to see what he had to say.

'Sorry, Soph, forgot to put this in the parcel.'

Dippy creative type.

'Just wanted to let you know I'm moving on.'

Well, duh, I thought, you do run a touring theatre company.

'We're taking the company to the Greek islands for the foreseeable future, to tour the expat communities there. Reckon that could become our permanent base.'

I didn't blame him. Better weather, better diet, cheaper wine.

'No idea of our address till we get there and find somewhere.'

Still, you know where I live, so it'll be easy to let me know as soon as you get there.

'I guess that's it. Over and out. Damian.'

So it was definitely over between us after all. Not that I really wanted it not to be. I slipped the postcard back into the letter cage, pretending to myself it had never arrived.

When I slumped down on the sofa, I saw the letter cage through Auntie May's eyes. I imagined how she must have felt whenever she saw the postman had delivered a new postcard from me – a short, non-committal message relaying bare facts about my travels; a meagre offering compared to the long, beautifully thought out letters that she sent to me in return. I'd given her a poor deal. I was as bad as Damian. I deserved his pathetic card.

But May was much smarter than me. Smart enough to recognise the young, brash, self-centred girl that I now saw myself to be. How did she come to be so wise? I suppose she was once one herself.

Damian's callous gesture forced my hand to go to the Wendlebury Players' meeting. Perhaps it wasn't the ideal route for me to find romance, given my history with Damian, but it seemed a more likely place to meet a new man than where I spent most of my time away from home: a bookshop run by a gay man and largely patronised by women, children and old men with a drink problem. At least at the Wendlebury Players I'd be able to talk the talk. I might get a part in the next play or even sell them one of my scripts.

How funny it would be if, after spending so long listening to

Damian discouraging me from writing on the basis that it wasn't a proper job, I penned a play that went on to become an internationally successful production. And Damian would have missed his chance to be my leading man and share the spoils. Wherever in Europe he ended up, I'd track him down via his drama company's website and make sure he knew what he'd missed.

So, on with the show, I told myself. But first, what to wear to a village drama club meeting? After another tussle with May's wardrobe, I decided to be brave and go as myself. At least then I wouldn't have to act. I hoped the Wendlebury Players members would be equally down to earth. I'd reserve judgement till I knew I could trust them.

18

STAGE FRIGHT

After fortifying myself with a small glass of wine from the fridge, I headed down to the Village Hall to join the Wendlebury Players' meeting about their autumn show, which was to be a historical drama. They seemed to have cast it already, so I was unlikely to get a part, but at least I could begin to make connections, building relationships in good time for the following production. Used to theatrical types, I thought I should be able to hold my own in a conversation with a bunch of provincial luvvies.

I strolled up the High Street to the Hall, saying the customary hello to everyone I encountered on the way, whether or not I knew who they were. This friendly habit had felt intrusive when I was staying with Auntie May as a shy teenager, but now I took it in my stride. It made me feel as if I was welcome and belonged to the community, as did the floral scents wafting towards me from the front gardens through the heavy early evening air, catching in the back of my throat. Passing by a vast mock orange bush next door to the Hall, I felt as if I'd been pollinated.

As I entered the Hall, I saw chairs arranged in a circle around the man I presumed to be Rex Hunter, the director. The occupants were all flicking through bound scripts, highlighter pens in hand, pouncing on their lines. They didn't seem to have started rehearsing yet. That made it easier for me to introduce myself without feeling I was interrupting.

Rex, the first to spot me, flashed me a smarmy smile. 'Well, hello there,' he said, channelling Leslie Phillips. 'What have we here?'

Everyone else looked up from their scripts, as if this was a spot-test of their powers of observation.

'Oh, I know her, Rex,' said a woman who looked vaguely familiar. 'Some apprentice teacher type. You're too late, darling, all the parts have been cast for this show.'

For a moment I couldn't place her, then her disdainful tone reminded me. It was Linda Absolom from the school office, the lady who thought herself too important for small change.

'I wasn't necessarily coming to audition for this show,' I explained. 'But I had been wondering whether I might join your company. I have a lot to offer.'

Shooting a look at Linda, which she met with a scowl, Rex stood up and held out his hand for me to shake. 'New actors are always welcome here.'

I stretched out my hand in return. His was uncomfortably warm and damp, and the minute I clasped it, he wrapped his other hand over the top, trapping mine and stroking it with the tips of his fingers. He gave me the creeps. I pulled my hand away as fast as I could without seeming rude. I'd met his kind before.

Another man in the mainly female group got up to fetch me a chair, and everyone scraped their seats along to make space for me to join their circle. He put the chair between Linda and Rex and beckoned to me to sit down. Quick as a flash, Linda moved along one to sit next to Rex, so I sat beside her instead. I don't think she realised how thankful I was.

'So what exactly can you add?' Linda sounded disdainful, addressing me but fixing Rex with a glare. 'I hear you're the tea lady in the bookshop now.'

I blushed, wondering how to answer that. Fortunately, everyone else ignored her. I got the impression they usually did.

'Do I gather you have experience in the theatre?' Rex asked, with a smile that didn't reach his eyes. I braced myself, not wanting to alienate him before I'd achieved what I'd come here for.

'Yes, I've been involved with a touring company in Europe for a number of years. And I'm keen on scriptwriting too. I'd be happy to write something specifically for your company, if you'd like me to, once I've got to know you.'

'Wonderful, darling.' Rex leaned across Linda to pat my knee. She drew back and gave his arm an admonishing slap, which I presumed she meant to look playful. 'It is such a chore to find a script that matches our particular cast and talents. Always risky to compromise.'

'And expensive,' put in a middle-aged woman who I presumed to be the group's treasurer.

Before he could probe further about my theatrical experience, I distracted him by going off at a tangent.

'My other reason for coming is that I've joined the Show Committee. I'm here to tell you that they're awfully keen for you to put in a float for the Show Carnival procession. We thought it might draw a bigger audience for your autumn show. Stanley can provide a trailer, and I'm sure we could find a four-by-four driver to tow it for you.'

'Hmm, not a bad idea,' said the treasurer lady. 'The fabric for Carol to make those lavish Tudor costumes will cost a fortune. We'll need every performance to be a sell-out, and a Saturday matinee too, to boost the takings.'

Murmurs of assent went around the group, with the odd proviso: 'So long as I can get up the showground first thing on Show Day to put my dahlias into the judging tent'; 'Provided we don't have to wear our costumes all day – I'm in the mums' tug-of-war in the afternoon'; 'Please say you won't make us wear stage make-up – it'll melt in that heat if it's the sunny weather we usually have on Show Day'. But what clinched it for Rex was talk of the trophy. He seemed the competitive type.

Linda was quick to lay down some ground rules.

'You can't possibly be on our float, Sophie. I think it should be the leading players only: Rex and his six wives.'

'Rex has six wives?' I gasped, before I could stop myself. He seemed the type to play the field, but this was ridiculous.

She fixed me with a sneer. 'Rex plays Henry VIII. I play Anne Boleyn.'

I bet there was no shortage of volunteers to play the executioner.

'And Ian,' said one of the other queens. 'We've got to have Ian, even though his is a non-speaking part.'

All the other ladies agreed, but I could see Rex wasn't keen to share the limelight with another man. I pretended not to be offended.

'Oh, that's fine. I've already agreed to be on the Wendlebury Writers' float.'

There, I thought, that'll compound my credibility as dramatist of their next play. Still, I couldn't complain. It had been easier than I'd expected to achieve both my objectives.

In spite of my misgivings about the odious Rex, I willingly accepted his invitation to stay to hear their read-through of the script. I thought it would help me get to know the actors' strengths and weaknesses, and give me ideas for the characters I could write for them in my play. By their tea break halfway through the evening, I'd relaxed so much that I even let Linda push me into the kitchen to serve the tea.

'That's what Sophie does for a living, you know,' she reminded everyone loudly. I resisted the temptation to spit in hers before I served it. I suspected I wouldn't be the first to have done so.

The treasurer lady, Mary, came in to help me wash the cups up after the break. Cast as Catherine of Aragon, she didn't appear in the second half of the play.

'Don't you mind Linda's remarks, she's just a bit possessive of Rex. They go back a long way. She knew him before he moved to the village, and before she was married. Not that she's married any more – not divorced yet, but it's in the pipeline. Her husband's run off with someone from work.' She leaned a bit closer to me confidentially, and giggled. I anticipated a juicy revelation. 'Apparently she used to be his lovely assistant when he was a professional conjuror. Can you imagine it?'

I smiled as I pictured the expensively-dressed Linda in a sparkly nylon leotard and ostrich feathers. It made her seem less scary.

'Not that they can be open about their affair, given that Rex already has a partner. He lives with a woman called Dido – or, by all accounts, lives off her. She's got some terrifically highly paid job in the City while he's just a part-time drama teacher at the local secondary school. She owns their house. Between you and me, if I were Dido, I'd chuck him out on his ear for carrying on.'

* * *

I walked home with a light and cheery tread, despite having been lumbered with a bag of used teabags to put on my compost heap at Rex's insistence. People were very conscientious about recycling in the village. I didn't like to tell him that I had yet to go near Auntie May's compost heap, expecting it to be repulsive, chucking all my waste in the wheelie bin. Hoping no-one saw me, I walked down the road carrying the bag as gingerly as if it was dog poo, but without the dog to justify it.

On going down to the bottom of the garden, I was pleasantly surprised to discover that compost heaps give off no smell at all. Well, who knew? I determined to make more use of mine in future. Joshua would be able to tell me what to do with the compost.

Afterwards, as I settled down on the sofa with pen and notebook in hand, I realised I had no idea as to what kind of play I should write for the Wendlebury Players. I ran through types that might suit their personalities. A bedroom farce? No, too close for comfort for Linda and Rex. A romantic comedy? Rex would certainly enjoy being the male lead. I decided to make Mary Rex's character's love interest to spite Linda, but then thought Mary wouldn't thank me for it.

I gathered I wasn't the only one made to feel uncomfortable in his presence, but I wasn't sure why. There was something unsettling about his exaggerated courtesy and charm. It spoke volumes about my relationship with Damian that a man being attentive and tactile would put me on my guard.

Damian again. He kept coming back to haunt me like Hamlet's ghost. Perhaps I should write a play about exorcism.

Feeling no further forward by bedtime, I determined to check the how-to section in Hector's House next day for books on playwriting, preferably while Hector wasn't looking.

19

DRUMROLL

Plenty of others were also consulting Hector's House, to help them prepare their Show entries. As Hector had predicted, sales of both gardening books and craft books crept up and up as Show Day got closer. Some of the books ordered filled me with surprise and intrigue – instruction manuals for crafts I'd never heard of and obscure specialist manuals devoted to a single vegetable or flower variety.

Not all of these sales led to show wins, or, Hector told me, even to show entries. Too often people's ambition outstripped the time they had to prepare their entries and they gave up as soon as they realised how much effort it really took to grow a prize marrow or bake an award-winning cake. Linda Absolom was one such, Hector said, having bought six different books about honey production the previous year, although she still hadn't got round to installing beehives in her garden.

I also noticed villagers becoming ever more secretive about the activities in their gardens.

We were lucky to be having a classic English summer, with glorious sunshine late into the evening and barely a breeze to cool you down, although the seasoned Show exhibitor would apparently have welcomed rain to spare them the daily task of watering fruit, vegetable and flowers by hand to avoid scorching or shrivelling. I had not appreciated until now how closely bound the growing of produce was with the vagaries of the English weather. A summer with a hosepipe ban was the second worst fear after a wet Show Day. It struck me that England wasn't the ideal country in which to stage traditional English village shows.

While I did not expect to enter any of the flowers or fruit from Auntie May's garden into the Show, I demonstrated kindred spirit by ostentatiously watering my flower beds, especially the more visible ones in the front garden, whenever I remembered. I wanted my new neighbours to realise I wasn't the townie igno- ramus they took me for.

Hector, whom I'd have thought would be pleased with the run on self-help books, alongside the flurry of bulk orders from schools as they prepared for the next academic year, became increasingly agitated. He spent more and more time at his computer, typing like a man possessed. At first, I thought this was to process all the orders, but then he started delegating those to me. He also showed me how to replenish the shelves as new deliveries arrived and how to remove the non-movers and return them to the publishers for credit. This heartless cull made me all the more anxious about my own prospects as an author. I hoped when my turn came, stockists would be more merciful.

In the meantime, I kept trying to find out exactly what Hector was typing. I assumed he was in some kind of financial trouble and consequently engaged in extensive correspondence with his creditors. Now that Auntie May was no longer around to under- write his debts, and his parents were living on a pension in a seaside bungalow, his business was terribly exposed. I could think of no other small village that sustained its own bookshop.

Even city centre bookstores, with their huge customer base, were closing down at an alarming rate. How on earth could Hector's House survive with its daily trickle of shoppers? I was torn between offering my resignation to ease his financial burden and dreading parting company from him, even though I knew he was unattainable to me, romantically speaking.

To assuage my conscience, and in hope of averting Hector's impending financial crisis, I tried to find other ways to increase the shop's sales. I worked late one night to surprise him with a spectacular window display on the theme of the Village Show, secretly borrowing toy trucks, tractors, Playmobil and Sylvanian characters from my pupils to create a little carnival procession running the width of the window. He was certainly surprised next morning, and at least the schoolchildren, winding home in the last few days of the school term, stopped to press their sticky noses against the glass each night, squabbling about which diminutive float should win first prize.

* * *

One afternoon, when Hector had gone to deliver books to a secondary school a few miles away, I took it into my head to inter-rogate his PC for clues about the precise nature of his problems. I called up the list of recent documents to see if there were any obvious suspects. The one he'd been updating before he went out was called 'A Lover's Revenge'. With my heart pounding, I clicked on the file to delve inside, but it was password protected.

I gasped and sat back on the stool. I didn't know Hector had a lover and wondered who he might be. There weren't any obvious candidates in the village at least – as Hector himself kept pointing out, there were no eligible single men close to my, or his, age, so perhaps he was involved with a much older man. I certainly hadn't spotted anyone in the shop whom Hector looked at in that particular way. He was affable, yet distant with almost everyone. Either he was being careful to cover his tracks, or his lover lived further afield.

I wondered whether it was one of the distant customers that he delivered to on his mysterious treks out when I was left to mind the shop. Of course, there was no reason it had to be anyone to do with the business at all. But why did he need to be so secretive?

I had a bad feeling about it.

Seeing him park his Land Rover on the street outside the shop, I hurriedly closed down Word, and determined to keep a special eye on his behaviour towards all his customers in future.

20

CARNIVAL TIME

For the next few weeks, there was plenty to distract me from identifying Hector's secret lover.

Preparing for Show Day seemed to have become everyone's priority. The next meeting of the Wendlebury Writers focused entirely on decorating our float. We talked about what we would wear and what props we would need. We each had to choose a book written by our proposed literary hero, preferably an edition that had their name in large print on the cover, visible from a distance, so that we could sit reading it on the float, to help people realise who we were meant to be. Finding the right period chairs for each author was more of a challenge. And we needed to decorate the float's backdrop to stand out in the judging.

This meeting was taking place in Hector's House, so I was able to persuade them to invest in twenty sheets of wrapping paper printed with the spines of old books. If we pasted all these on to the backboard of the float, it would look like we were in an old-fashioned library.

'Better coat it with plenty of yacht varnish,' said Dinah. 'Just in case the heavens open upon us.'

In addition, we met every few days in one of Stanley's barns, where our trailer lay waiting for us. We pasted up our library-effect wallpaper on a backboard, carpeted the floor with old rugs, and hung bunting made out of the pages of old books. Unwilling to cut up perfectly good books, I'd approached a local charity shop and discovered that in their backroom they had more donated copies of *Fifty Shades of Grey* than they could ever hope to sell, so they gave them to us for free. It was a good thing the bunting was high up along the top of the trailer, so that no-one in the crowd would be able to read it.

When the float was complete, we had an entertaining meeting back at Hector's House reading the opening chapters aloud from each of the books we'd chosen for our characters, followed by a show of hands to vote for the best, like a lazy person's balloon debate. I read from Auntie May's ancient hardback of Woolf's *To the Lighthouse*, pleased to think that a little piece of May was still taking part in the Show.

Finally we had a dress rehearsal to try out our proposed costumes and practise our hairstyles to suit our characters.

This flurry of activity was all handy for me, because it postponed the day when I had to bring some of my own writing for the group to critique. I was hoping I could get away with it until I'd actually written something worth sharing.

The night before the show I barely slept at all, fearful of oversleeping and missing the start of the procession. I also wanted to make sure I had plenty of time to arrange my hair in Virginia Woolf's characteristic style and practise my pose. I drank plenty of water and ate a good breakfast at the insistence of Barbara Cartland, who reminded me that if the weather continued to be so hot, it could become a strain on the system. Standing around on a hot float waiting for the judging, we could too easily, she said, become dehydrated or weak with hunger.

Little did I know that food and drink would be the least of my Show Day problems.

21

BEST DAY OF THE YEAR

I could hardly eat my breakfast for excitement. Posing before the wardrobe mirror in my Virginia Woolf costume, I looped my hair into a low bun, then walked carefully in my kitten-heeled shoes up to the Village Green to take my place on our float.

Hector had already arrived, having towed the float up from Stanley's barn with his Land Rover, but I hardly recognised him. I hadn't expected him to dress up too. He wore a white toga, baring one taut shoulder and downy calves. His flesh was firmer and more muscular than one might expect for someone who spent his working days sitting behind a desk, tapping at a keyboard. In the sunshine instead of our shady shop, with its small windows fronting on to the High Street, he looked fresher faced and more energised.

He caught me looking. 'Homer. No, not Simpson, before you ask. The proper one.'

He certainly looked at home as Homer. I was glad he never wore his toga to work, or I'd not get any work done. I wished I'd picked a more flattering costume. With my plain hairstyle, no make-up, and a dress that flattened rather than enhanced any curves, I looked like a charmless bluestocking.

But of course, after what Carol had told me, I knew he could never be interested in me as anything other than an employee, or, best case, as a friend. What with him and Damian, I berated myself, I really was very bad at picking men.

I was surprised he hadn't said he was going to dress up when I'd told him the characters the rest of the group were playing. Speaking of which, these were all now gravitating towards us from the different directions of their homes around the village.

Hector offered his hand to help us balance as we climbed aboard to take our seats, starting with Barbara Cartland. Resplendent in pink chiffon, she took her place in a high-backed velveteen armchair. Although still in her thirties, Karen didn't need to put much thought into her costume, because she usually wore pink anyway. Far prettier than the real Barbara Cartland, she'd had the good sense not to cover up her classic English rose complexion with Cartlandesque pancake make-up. She looked like the innocent heroine of one of her own romantic stories, published by the kind of women's magazines that never mention sex. They were the perfect antidote to an overdose of *Cosmopolitan*.

We had just taken our places on the float when Trevor dashed over to remind us to register our presence at the judges' table. We all climbed down again and trooped over to sign the list.

'You were meant to collect your float number last night too,' said Trevor, handing a numbered card to Hector to put on his windscreen. 'If you don't have it, you won't know which order to line up in. You don't want to confuse the judges.'

'Honestly, it's not as if anyone could get any of our floats mixed up,' huffed Dinah, casting a withering glance at the Gardening Club's array of human scarecrows.

When we returned to the float no more than five minutes later, we were horrified to discover that in our absence some anonymous joker had sneaked onto our float to execute a string of practical jokes. Agatha Christie (Louisa) discovered a sticker on the back of her cane chair saying 'The butler did it'. On the long tail of Charles Dickens's black coat, draped over her high bentwood stool, was a pink Post-it note enquiring 'Who the Dickens is she meant to be?' Admittedly Jacky, the local dentist, a slim and feminine figure, did look a little unlikely in her false beard.

A vulgar limerick had been tucked under the collar of the toy dog that was waiting to go on Elizabeth Barrett Browning's lap. It didn't have to be very near the knuckle to offend our sweet and gentle poetess, Jessica. Robert Frost (Bella, Parish Clerk) found on her seat a plastic rose, to which was sellotaped a note saying 'A pose is a pose and is always a pose'. Receiving a rose in any other context would have been a compliment, but this felt like a threat.

Julia, the high school history teacher, found a message on Jean Plaidy's stool saying 'You're history, sweetheart'. She admitted to being the victim of worse jokes in the classroom. The joke played on Sylvia Plath, aka Dinah, was more erudite, and crueller. The caption 'It's a gas' had been sellotaped to her plastic kitchen chair.

But it was my own fate that most upset me. When I picked up Virginia Woolf's long cardigan from my low leather pouffe, its pockets were full of stones.

Dinah refused to let us dwell on the matter, briskly tearing up the notes and handing the scraps of paper to me to dispose of.

'There's no time to discuss this now. Places, ladies.'

Not wanting to miss the off, I stuffed the paper into the copious pockets of my dress, then returned the stones from my cardigan pockets to the drive from which they'd clearly been taken. Then we took our seats and assumed our planned literary poses. While we awaited the arrival of the judges, I couldn't help but wonder who the joker was.

The only one of our group to be left unscathed was Barbara Cartland, who in literary terms was arguably the most deserving of disdain. Could Karen have been the culprit? Was some weird Jekyll-and-Hyde character hiding beneath her sweet and gentle exterior?

Whoever the perpetrator, he or she had more than a passing knowledge of our authors' lives, including the fact that Sylvia Plath had committed suicide by putting her head in a gas oven and Virginia Woolf by filling her pockets with rocks and drowning herself in a river. I noticed Dinah glaring accusingly, first at the scarecrows then at Rex, smug as Henry VIII on the Wendlebury Players' float. But Dinah looks daggers at most men, most of the time, so I didn't read anything into it.

Surely it had not been Hector? He was meant to be on our side. Besides, his sense of humour was more mature. He might have had the opportunity to slip these items into place, having accessed the float before our arrival, but what could his motive have been? Revenge for being volunteered as our driver? He'd seemed happy enough to get involved when I suggested it. He'd even entered into the spirit by dressing up.

I glanced across to where he was standing by the Land Rover, putting off the moment of getting back into the hot cab. His toga was an enviably cool and comfortable outfit for this scorcher of a day, and it showed off his shapely legs a treat. I found myself wondering whether the ancient Greeks took the same approach to underwear as kilted Scotsmen.

The judges were approaching.

'Don't be put off,' hissed Dinah to the rest of us. 'That's exactly what the wretched prankster wants. Hold your positions, ladies!'

The judging complete, the vehicles revved their engines,

ready to progress to the Show Ground where the winners would be announced. As our float bumped slowly down the High Street behind the Players', we tried to look as if we were contemplating the muse, undistracted by less noble thoughts.

In front of the procession of floats walked dozens of children and adults in fancy dress costume. Leading them was Joshua, who'd performed this duty for more than forty years. When he first told me about it, I'd queried the need to have a navigator for the carnival when it only travelled a few hundred metres from the Village Green to the recreation ground on a straight road with no junctions, but I'd regretted asking as soon as I'd understood how much the position meant to him. Everyone had their favourite role to play on Show Day. The sense of community that bound us was almost palpable. There was so much to observe and take in. Like any aspiring writer, I'm a natural people watcher, but I quickly reached sensory overload.

The High Street was lined three or four people deep on either side. Their enjoyment as they watched us trundle past helped abate the bitter taste of the pranks. After all, the perpetrator hadn't done us physical harm, just taken the edge off our excitement.

When we reached the showground's arena, delineated by bales of straw on which the crowds following us now made themselves comfortable, our drivers lined our floats up next to each other ready for the announcement of the winners. We parked alongside the Wendlebury Players' float, and the WI's pulled up alongside us. The nail-biting wait began to see which carnival floats had won prizes.

Little did we know that within a quarter of an hour, the announcement of the winners would be eclipsed by the news that Henry VIII was down to five wives.

22

THE SHOW MUST GO ON

Poor Linda. I may not have liked her much, but I wouldn't have wished her dead. Nor would I have thought her a likely candidate to die a premature death. A more aged actress might have been pleased to die treading the boards on a mobile stage, but Linda was only in her forties. She had seemed perfectly healthy when I'd first met her a few weeks before. Surely no-one terminally ill would have had enough energy to be so cross all the time?

Intimidated by the crowd of people gathering around her, I climbed back up onto our float. From there I could see the St John Ambulance edging its way towards us from the other end of the field. Aware of my responsibilities as the newest member of the Show Committee, I called out in my best teacher's voice: 'Please stand back. Make way for the paramedics.'

Several heads swivelled angrily towards me.

'She's my neighbour.'

'I'm her husband.'

'She's my mum.'

I was mortified. I was so used to living at a distance from my family that it hadn't occurred to me that Linda's would be in the crowd. Even her estranged husband had returned to the village for Show Day. For a moment, his look of distress was supplanted by rage, as if I'd just struck Linda down dead myself. Then he turned back to her body, stroking her face, murmuring, 'My darling, I'm so sorry.'

Hector appeared quietly beside me and grasped my elbow. I jumped at his unexpected touch.

'Come on, you. Listen to the wise words of Homer. Let's go and get a cup of tea.'

My knight in shining toga. When I leaned heavily against him, he put his arm around me and led me down the steps off the float. As we wove through the crowd, I wished my face, now scarlet with embarrassment, had been covered by my costume, like Anne Boleyn's. By the time we reached the Village Hall, I was sobbing with a mixture of vicarious grief for Linda's family and remorse for piling on the hurt with my misplaced remark. I concluded that I'd have to leave the village as rapidly as I'd arrived. Surely they'd all hate me now. How could I have been so stupid?

Then a Keystone Kop pushed past me, heading down to the arena. I wiped my eyes, wondering whether the shock was making me hallucinate, and turned to Hector for an explanation.

'Didn't you recognise Bob?' asked Hector. 'You know, from the Show Committee? He always dresses like that on Show Day.'

'What Bob the bobby? Yes, of course.' I blinked to focus through my tears, thankful for a nanosecond of comic relief. But then a dreadful thought occurred to me for the first time. I wasn't just dreadfully embarrassed, I was guilty of cold-blooded murder.

'Wait, Hector! I think you should call Bob back.' I waved my arms in the direction of the Keystone Kop. 'I've just realised, I have a confession to make.'

Hector stopped abruptly in the middle of the busy thoroughfare and stared at me in surprise. 'He's a policeman, not a priest. Whatever do you want to confess?'

I put my hands over my face and bowed my head. 'It's a policeman that I need, Hector. Because, don't you see? I killed Linda Absolom!'

He grabbed my arm and steered me across to stand by the wall, where it was marginally quieter.

'Whatever do you mean, Sophie?'

I dropped my hands and gazed at him, my eyes full of tears. 'I killed Linda. It's all my fault that she went on that wretched float, because I asked the Wendlebury Players to join the carnival. If I hadn't persuaded Rex that it was a good idea, Linda would still be alive. Don't you see that?'

Hector gave a wry smile and drew me into his arms for a comforting hug – the hug of a friend. Platonic. I suppose I should call it Homeric really.

'It's not your fault at all, you daft thing. It's not as if you made her take up skydiving. Sitting on a carnival float is a very, very safe activity. She did it of her own free will, and no-one in their wildest dreams would blame you that she happened to die on it. You've just had a nasty shock, and you're letting your imagination run away with you. Come and have a cup of tea, and once I've moved our float out of the arena, I'll meet you down in the beer tent and buy you a glass of something stronger.'

With one arm still around me, Hector guided me into the hall and over to a table where Sylvia Plath was filling enough mismatched china cups for all our group from a large aluminium teapot.

'I'll leave you in Dinah's capable hands.'

'Please, Hector, can't you stay with me for a bit?'

Even though I knew he wasn't interested in women, I'd been

enjoying the feel of his arm around me, the edge of his toga brushing against my bare arm. Despite my distress, I couldn't help wondering whether he'd made his toga out of his bedsheets.

'No, I really must get our float out of the arena now the judging's been done. They'll be wanting the space for the entertainments programme. I think the sheepdog demonstration is due to begin any minute now.'

'What? Won't they cordon off the arena for forensic investigations?'

'I don't think so, Sophie. It's clearly natural causes. It's not as if blood has been spilled, or there are murder weapons about the place. Well, not real ones, anyway. Ian's axe is only cardboard.' He looked up at the sky. 'Good thing it didn't rain.'

'But won't they at least cancel the rest of the Show out of respect for the dead?'

''Fraid not. Miss Plath will explain, won't you, Dinah?'

As if I were a baton she'd been handed, Dinah, strangely unmoved by Linda's demise, took charge of me, and Hector strode out of the Hall.

'The Show must go on, Sophie, as Linda would have been the first to insist. There are too many people with too much riding on today to cancel the event when it's barely begun. There'd be a riot. Just think of all those stallholders, the dog trainers and the dancers waiting to perform in the arena, not to mention the kids who look forward to Show Day all year round. Don't worry, it's not as bad as you might think. They'll name a cup in her honour next year, you wait and see.'

'A cup? What for? Best Murder in Show?' I asked.

Louisa busy removing hairpins and side combs to let down her Agatha Christie curls, paused for a moment.. 'Of course not. Whatever makes you think it was murder? It's not as if there was any blood or obvious murder weapons on the scene. She's just died of natural causes. It was only a matter of time before someone dropped dead at the Show. We all have to die sometime, and when we have so many people in one place, it's a statistical fact that sooner or later it'll coincide with somebody's last day on earth.. It'll turn out to be heatstroke, I expect, poor soul.'

She shook her head hard, like a wet dog, releasing the talcum powder with which she'd turned her hair grey. A cloud of lily of the valley rose up around her, settling over the Bourbon biscuits.

'Like with cruise ships,' put in Julia, offering me the biscuit plate. 'You always expect a few dead bodies by the end of a cruise, because they carry so many old people. They even have purpose-built morgues in modern cruise ships.'

'Ugh, I think I'll stick to camping,' said Bella, wiping Robert Frost's five o'clock shadow off on a paper serviette 'Anyway, Sophie, we're not being as disrespectful as you might think. It's a real honour to have a cup named after you. Makes you immortal, as it gets your name mentioned on Show Day for ever more.

I clasped my hands around my teacup for comfort before venturing a question. 'Weren't any of you friends with Linda? Didn't you at least like her?'

They briefly exchanged glances, as if wondering who should be the first to confess. Inevitably it was Dinah.

'Nope. I'm not sure she had close friends. She never really worked at actual friendship. Tried to force herself on lots of people by sucking up to them, or bossing them about, pushing things on them, moulding them to herself, but it didn't cut both ways. Offered me a fashion makeover, for example. Tried to persuade me to dye my hair and start wearing make-up. I ask you!' She tutted.

'And she gave me a diet book,' said Jessica, whose eyeliner was smudged with tears as she reached for another slice of Victoria sponge. 'And she tried to make me adopt one of her unwanted kittens. She didn't consider for a moment that my Charlie wouldn't have liked it at all.'

'I don't think I've met your husband,' I said. 'I didn't know you were married.'

'Charlie's not my husband. He's my King Charles Spaniel.'

'Oh, I'm sure she meant well, Dinah,' put in Karen. 'Poor Linda. Perhaps her intentions were of the best.'

'You always were an optimist. That's how you can write romance without throwing up,' said Dinah. 'I'm more of a realist. Now, let's put this unpleasantness behind us. *Carpe diem*. Because Show *Diem* only comes once a year.'

After that, we barely talked about the pranks, for which I was truly grateful, though Dinah made a damning observation before the subject was dropped.

'What I don't understand is how anyone could have known in advance which authors we would play, so that they could prepare the right labels. But everyone knows we all keep our costumes a secret till Show Day. I don't get it.'

So now the pranks were my fault too. I tried to remember whom I'd told – Hector, obviously, but that didn't seem unreasonable considering he was towing our float.

Then I thought of Carol.

Oh God, Carol! Another thought struck me, too terrible to speak of. Carol was the Players' wardrobe mistress. Had she designed Linda's costume to suffocate her? I was relieved to remember that I'd seen Linda striding about in it for twenty minutes before she got on the float, posing for photographs and startling old ladies in the crowd. She couldn't have done that without being able to breathe.

But with access to everyone's prescription medicines in the shop, Carol might easily have slipped Linda a drugged drink designed to kill her in costumed sight. She'd even stitched Linda into her dress to keep her trapped while it did its work.

Could Carol's jealousy of Linda's relationship with Rex have led her to murder?

23

A NEW LIGHT

Half an hour later, I stepped back out onto the Recreation Ground, awash with tea and on a sugar rush from being fed too many biscuits. Hector was slowly driving across the car park, towing our float. I flagged him down and ran round to the driver's side, where he'd wound down the window because of the heat.

'Is it safe to go back to the arena now?' I asked him.

'They've carted Linda's body off in the ambulance, if that's what you mean,' he said, reading me like a book. Well, he is a bookseller. 'But I tell you what' – he gestured to me to move in closer – 'I just heard one of the St John Ambulance men in the arena saying he thought she had severe heat rash, so maybe the costume was the cause. Though why Catherine Howard didn't have the same problem is a mystery. Their costumes were almost identical. But keep that to yourself. We don't want to upset anyone with speculation till the post-mortem result comes through. There's enough gossip in this village without starting up more. For now, let's enjoy the Show.'

He looked at his watch, breaking his Homeric spell for a moment.

'I'll be back when I've parked the Land Rover behind the shop. Go and cheer yourself up by having a good look round the exhibition tent. It'll be spectacular, I promise you. I'll come and find you later.'

And with that he put his car into gear and pulled away, the trailer rattling behind him as he turned onto the High Street.

Not wanting to appear needy, I decided to check out the exhibits. Hector was right: the marquee *was* spectacular. I spent at least an hour wandering round in the surreal world of marrows the size of toddlers and runner beans like walking sticks. I'd have an awful lot of questions to ask Joshua and Hector later.

The marquee certainly provided me with the opportunity to view my new neighbours in a different light. Although all the exhibits were submitted anonymously, once the judging was over, the names of the winners were revealed. I was startled to discover that a number of villagers whom I'd put down as being uninteresting or untalented had remarkable gifts, from intricate embroidery and cake decoration to mammoth marrows and plums too perfect to be true. They were of course all truly the work of the entrants. As a member of the Show Committee, I had learned that any exhibitor would be disqualified if discovered submitting work that was not their own. The committee reserved the right to inspect the gardens of anyone whom they suspected of fraud. I wondered how many times this right had been exercised.

When I emerged, blinking, into the afternoon sunshine, I spotted a man on the Suffragettes' float, sawing away at their chains with a huge metal file. None of the WI had been able to find the key, so their driver had had to move their float out of the arena with them all still aboard. People were now queuing up with a series of tools to cut through the metal. I wondered how the women could have been daft enough to mislay their key. I supposed they were at the age where their memories were starting to play up.

Then I remembered that apart from the biscuits, I'd eaten nothing since breakfast, so I went to join the queue for the deer roast – perfect for lining my stomach before tracking down Hector in the beer tent. I had to force myself to do my bit to support the Show, despite my growing anxieties about my safety in the village.

24

THE SPOILS OF THE SHOW

Despite Dinah's assurances, I was astonished at how readily everyone allowed the show to continue normally. I wondered whether they all knew about Linda's death. No one had thought fit to announce it over the tannoy. I supposed it might have caused panic and confusion in between shout-outs for lost children and husbands.

After I'd finished my deer roast sandwich, I ambled around the stalls for an hour, buying raffle and tombola tickets to support the local charities running them, and trying my hand at fairground favourites such as Splat the Rat and the coconut shy. I didn't think anyone still did coconut shies, but this one seemed to bring out the competitive instinct in men of all ages. Some of the women proved a dab hand at it too.

I watched Rex showing off to the crowd with a volley of accurate shots. After what the others had said over tea, I shouldn't have been surprised that he was still at the show, but considering the tragedy had been on his float, involving the woman with whom we assumed he was having an affair, I found his absorption in his current task heartless. Perhaps it was just displacement activity for grief.

'What on earth will Rex do with seven coconuts?' I wondered aloud as I watched him from the sidelines.

'Juggle?' said Hector, materialising at my elbow. 'Pull rabbits out of them?'

'Or make them disappear,' said Carol, sidling up to Hector. Before I could stop myself, I'd taken a couple of steps back, suddenly nervous in her presence. She smiled at me appreciatively, assuming I was just letting her get closer to Hector. It seemed she hadn't given up on him romantically yet. 'He's very good, you know. He was showing me the other day how easy it is for shoplifters to smuggle things out without paying. It was quite an eye-opener, I can tell you. I don't know why he stopped being a magician, because he's really very good with – what do they call it? – spite of hand. It's not magic at all, of course. I might have to start frisking him before he leaves the shop in future.'

Her wistful expression suggested she would find that task no hardship. At that point, Hector did his own vanishing act. To my surprise, I spotted a hint of lust as Carol stared after him mingling with the crowd at the raffle stall. Talk about fickle. Show Day was clearly bringing out the beast in her.

'Why's Hector wearing a dress?' she asked abruptly.

'He's being Homer, the Greek poet,' I explained. She nodded sagely.

'Ah well, that would explain it. I suppose it's one way of advertising his romantic status. I mean, the Greeks invented it, didn't they?'

'Invented what?'

'Homersexuality.'

Suppressing a laugh, I changed the subject, leading the conversation off to probe about Rex's interesting former career as a cabaret magician. Now there was a ladies' man if ever there was one, apparently with no shortage of lovely assistants.

'When he first moved here, he planned to set himself up as a children's party conjuror, on the side from his drama teaching,' said Carol. 'But that never got off the ground. I don't know why. But don't listen to me, my dear. You know I'm not one to gossip. You want to ask the one person in the village that knew him back in his conjuring days.'

'Who would that be?' I asked, determined to do so.

'Why, Linda Absolom, of course!' she said brightly, before the events of earlier caught up with her. 'Oh dear. It's too late for that now, isn't it?'

Then she turned and scurried off to admire the exhibits for one last time before the tent was cleared at the end of the day. I'd seen her name on several winning entries in the floral art section. I couldn't blame her for wanting to prolong her moment of glory.

* * *

At around 5 p.m. I bumped into Barbara Cartland in the beer tent.

'I've had enough,' she said. 'I feel emotionally drained after this business with Linda. I know I didn't much like her, but still. It doesn't feel respectful to hang around getting drunk in the beer tent.'

She nodded towards Sylvia Plath, who was tucking into a pint of Guinness. It didn't look as if it was her first. She had her arm around another lady whom I didn't know, who was drinking Chardonnay from a full-sized bottle through a straw.

Just then, Rex brushed past me, and I noticed a small silver key drop from his codpiece. I didn't know codpieces were lock-able, and wondered idly whether it was the medieval feminist's answer to a chastity belt. Knowing Rex's reputation as a womaniser, perhaps Dido had insisted. I bent to pick it up, wondering whether I should return it to Dido rather than Rex, but was distracted by Hector's reappearance at my side.

'Like to come to the auction with me?'

I'd already learned from the Show Committee that the auction was the sale of exhibits donated by entrants at the end of the day. It raised funds towards the Show's running costs. These were higher than I'd realised, what with insurance and marquee hire, entertainments fees and prize money. The auction sounded like good fun, so I accepted Hector's invitation, wishing it wasn't a Platonic date. Oh, that toga!

The bidding, lubricated by the beer tent, was fast and furious. Many people went home with more goods than they could comfortably carry. Determined to enter into the spirit of it like a real villager, after a glass or two of warm white wine from the beer tent, I got stuck into the bidding. An hour later, when it was all over, I took home three heads of celery, four of lettuce, another jar of jam to add to Auntie May's collection, a less than successful loaf of white bread, a basket of small floral arrangements, and the makings of a hangover for next morning.

* * *

As I sipped my hot chocolate in bed, I tried to put the best complexion on the day's events. Without Linda's death, I would have had a marvellous time, except for those stupid pranks. I couldn't believe I'd got so het up about them now. After all, they paled into insignificance besides Linda's death. Or were they connected? Were they just harmless jokes in bad taste, or were they more sinister? Might Linda's death have been a prank that got out of hand?

Swirling the rest of my drink around in the mug, I watched

the remaining liquid pick up the foam from the rim of the cup. If she'd been in good health, being inside a warm costume for a couple of hours wouldn't have finished her off. Catherine Howard lived to tell the tale. Maybe Linda had been ill all along, but hadn't liked to mention it to anyone, especially if she had no close friends in the village. Perhaps she would turn out to have had a congenital heart disorder, or an aneurysm waiting to happen any time. Dinah was probably right. After the post-mortem pronounced death from natural causes, her family would hold the funeral, and we'd all feel better. Except Linda, of course.

As darkness fell, I became less sure. If there was a murderer at large, mightn't they strike again? I shivered, knocked back the rest of my cocoa, stood the empty mug on the bedside table, and snuggled down beneath the duvet.

My last thought before I drifted off to sleep was Damian's voice saying, 'You'll be murdered in your bed and nobody will be there to hear you scream.'

25

DEBRIEFING JOSHUA

The first thing I was aware of next morning was a loud banging sound. I thought it was inside my head, the result of too many plastic glasses of wine in the beer tent after the auction, until I realised it was coming from downstairs. Someone was hammering on the front door.

In broad daylight, the sound was far less scary than it would have been the night before. I staggered out of bed and lifted the sash window to see who it was. Leaning out, I saw Carol gently tapping with the brass knocker.

'Hang on, I'll be down in a sec,' I called. She looked up and waved when she spotted me.

'Sorry, I didn't realise you'd still be in bed.'

I stumbled into my slippers, trudged down the stairs and hauled the front door open. The sunshine struck me as very bright for so early in the day, till I glanced at my watch and saw it was gone eleven.

'Come in for some elevenses?' I offered weakly. I showed her through to the kitchen, where I filled the kettle from the tap and got out the makings of instant coffee.

'I wanted to thank you for bidding so much for my flowers last night at the auction,' Carol began. 'That was kind of you.'

'Not at all. They're lovely. Much nicer than a lot of other things I might have bid for. I don't suppose I can interest you in some celery? I have plenty,' I remembered. 'I thought I'd take the little jars of flowers to Hector's House tomorrow for the tearoom tables. I get a bit of hay fever, so probably best not to keep them all.'

'Good idea,' said Carol cheerily. 'They'll be good for local eco – enviro – good for the insects and birds.'

For someone who had possibly just committed a murder, she was remarkably bright and breezy. Did she have no conscience, no remorse? I didn't want her to know of my suspicions and was glad of the flowers as a talking point to keep the conversation going.

'Lovely for humans to look at, too. You ought to sell them in the shop, you know. Though people might not buy big fancy arrangements, I'm sure you could do those little bunches at an affordable price.'

'Do you think so? I've never thought of it before. Rex insisted on making up those little hanging flower balls to go with the queen costumes. He said they added an extra touch of authenticity. Apparently Tudor ladies used to carry flowers to stop them smelling bad, in the days before baths caught on. I have to say, having stitched all those ladies into the costumes on such a hot day, I began to see their point.'

I went cold, although my hands were round her hot mug of coffee. I set it down on the table in front of her, then picked up mine and hung on to it with both hands lest she'd come on a mission to drug it. No point putting temptation in her way.

I vaguely recalled learning about Tudor life in school history lessons. 'I thought it was plague that they were trying to ward off.'

'I think we can safely assume that Linda Absolom didn't die of plague,' said Carol. She reached over to the box of flowers and pulled out one little ball of blooms that hung from a scarlet ribbon. 'This was her posy.'

I stared at it askance, feeling deeply uncomfortable about its presence in my kitchen. It no longer seemed as pretty as before; I felt like I'd stolen a wreath from a grave. While I didn't want to hurt Carol's feelings, I determined to get rid of it as soon as we'd analysed the rights and wrongs of who won the prizes at the Show and she'd gone.

* * *

I finally got dressed around noon, after carefully hanging my Virginia Woolf dress up in the wardrobe once I'd found where I'd left it the night before: in a heap on the bathroom floor. I'd enjoyed being a bluestocking for the day, and I hoped I'd have the chance to wear it again soon.

As I came back downstairs to the kitchen, wondering whether I could yet stomach any toast, I saw Joshua approaching the back door. When I let him in, he sat down at the kitchen table, admiring the home-made bread and jam that lay next to my auction haul.

'Been baking this morning, have you?' He knew the answer already. I cut a slice of bread for him to sample and spread it with some of the jam, giving it a miss myself. The scarlet jam, which had not set properly, reminded me too much of blood, and of poor Linda. I knew this was irrational, because her blood had not been spilled.

'They're pretty,' said Joshua, noticing the box of flowers once he'd finished his first mouthful.

'Yes, Carol did them. Did you see how many awards she won

yesterday for flower arranging? She took the overall trophy for Best Floral Art too. I told her she ought to sell little arrangements like this in the shop. It's not as if she'd have to buy any materials, because she's got a garden full of flowers. I remember visiting it with Auntie May when I was little.'

'Hector told me you've got an eye for business.'

'Ha, he keeps saying that, but usually he passes his ideas off as mine. It's kind of him, but I'm not sure I deserve it.'

'Oh, just humour him,' said Joshua. 'I'm sure his intentions are of the best.'

'But what about these flowers? I'm not sure it's right to have Anne Boleyn's flowers here when Linda's lying dead in a hospital mortuary.' Gingerly I picked up her posy with a tea towel. 'I'm not superstitious, but I don't feel comfortable with them in the house.'

'Why not hang them up on that basket hook outside?' Joshua pointed to a wrought iron curlicue outside the window. 'I meant to tell you, I took down May's hanging baskets after she died as she'd not got round to planting them. They looked so desolate, hanging empty there. They're in her garden shed if you want them.'

I stood on the bench outside the window to put the flower ball on the wall hook. The ribbons fluttered in the light midday breeze. A sprinkle of rain overnight had freshened the air agreeably. I was feeling a little better.

'So what do you think about Linda's death?' I asked Joshua on my return. 'Do you think it was natural causes?'

I watched him carefully, thinking that if he was involved, he would be cautious in his response.

Joshua looked at me reproachfully. 'Why shouldn't it be? Young people die too.'

'She wasn't exactly young. She was in her forties.'

Joshua chuckled into his tea. 'My dear, when you're my age, forties seem like childhood. Why are you so convinced it may not be the case? Did you see anything suspicious?'

'Not exactly suspicious,' I began, and explained about the pranks on our float, wondering what he would make of them. I'd realised that although he was physically frail, his mind was razor sharp.

'Everyone's in high spirits on Show Day, so there's bound to be a little mischief. And it was mischief, not malice, even though not in the best of taste.'

I supposed he was right. 'But why did no-one seem upset about Linda's death?'

Another reproachful look. 'My dear, if you had seen her family leaving the showground, you wouldn't have said that. Even her estranged husband was distraught, though they parted months ago. He's been living in town for months, only returning for high days and holidays. Still working on their divorce settlement, apparently, so I suppose that's at least one blessing to come of it – no more haggling over access to the children. Dear me. I was raised in an age before divorce, you know.'

After a moment's silent thought, he pressed his hands down on the table to help him stand up, and rose to head for the door. 'Now, I'll leave you in peace, but don't forget to water Carol's beautiful flowers before the sun gets too high in the sky. And you keep that imagination of yours in check, my girl.'

I spent the rest of the day pottering quietly about the house, rehydrating and regaining my appetite. Towards mid-afternoon I noticed I was also spending a lot of time sneezing. Some of Carol's arrangements contained flowers that had an irritating fragrance. Natural scents – or a sign of poison? I immediately banished the rest of them to the garden, just in case.

Hooking a floral ball either side of the front door, where I remembered Auntie May used to hang baskets of geraniums each summer, I thought of Linda lying cold, and shivered.

* * *

I'd just come in from suspending the other garlands from low branches of the apple tree in the back garden when there was a hammering at my front door. This time, it really was hammering, not Carol's gentle tapping amplified by my hangover.

Gosh, I'm popular today, I thought, feeling more cheerful by now and hoping it might be Hector's turn to visit. Then I spotted Rex's distinctive slicked back hairstyle through the small glass window in the door.

He leapt forward as I opened it. 'What on earth do you think you're doing?' he snapped, startling me.

I stepped back. 'I'm not doing anything. Why?'

He pointed at the floral balls hanging either side of me.

'What are you doing with these?'

I explained that I'd bought them at the Show auction as a job lot. I hadn't realised till I got them home that they were from the Players' float; I'd thought they were part of the floral entries section.

'You can't have them. They're Carol's. She made them for me. Do you have all six? I've come to take them back to her.'

I shrugged. I was damned if I was going to be neighbourly and invite him in when he was being so rude, whether or not he was prospective director of my drama script.

'Carol doesn't want them. At least, she never asked me for them when she dropped by this morning. In fact, she positively thanked me for buying them in aid of the Show funds. She was flattered that I'd paid so much for them.'

'She should have asked me first. I commissioned her to make them for me, as part of my queens' costumes.'

'Did you pay her for them?' I congratulated myself on my quick thinking.

'No, not exactly, but the transaction was understood.'

'Not by Carol. She put them in the auction when she was clearing away your show float. Which you failed to do, by all accounts, leaving the hard work to Carol and Ian.'

He clapped a hand to his forehead in sudden horror.

'My God, she didn't auction off the dresses too, did she?'

I sighed. 'No, of course not. She's not stupid. She knows the dresses are needed for your autumn production. I saw her putting them back in the drama cupboard at the Village Hall. Some of them, anyway. I assume they carried poor Linda off in hers to the hospital. But it's not as if the flowers would last till autumn, is it?'

'Still, I demand to have my flowers back. All six of the arrangements.'

My head had started pounding again, making me lose my cool. 'Why, do you want one for each of your girlfriends? Or are you giving all six to Dido?'

Out of the corner of my eye, I noticed a movement to my left. Joshua was peering out of his front window, looking slightly anxious on my behalf. With an effort, he raised his sash window and called out.

'Pipe down, there, will you, and let a man have his Sunday afternoon nap in peace?'

Rex swivelled round to address Joshua. 'I've only come to ask for what's rightfully mine. I don't know why you have to interfere, you silly old fool.'

Rex clearly saved all his charm for his women.

'Oh for goodness' sake, man, pull yourself together! What's got into you? Someone stolen your magic wand?' Joshua chuckled, completely unaffected by Rex's bluster. 'White rabbit escaped from your hat?'

Rex scowled. 'My flowers. I've come for the Players' flowers.'

He pointed to the posies swinging gently in the growing breeze.

'I think you'll find in law they belong to Sophie now, given that she paid for them in public view, and that their maker is happy with the transaction. If Carol wants to change her mind and ask for them back, that's down to her.'

'We'll soon see about that!' snapped Rex. He turned and marched off down the path and back up the High Street.

I climbed over the low dry stone wall that separated Auntie May's front path from Joshua's to speak to him in confidence.

'Thanks for coming to my rescue. I can't believe how nasty that man can be. And to think I've offered to write him a free play. Talk about ingratitude!'

'No wonder he and Linda got on so well,' replied Joshua. 'Two peas in a pod when it comes to temper.'

'Really? He's the only person I've come across so far who hadn't fallen out with her. I'm surprised he wasn't more upset when they found she was dead.'

'Oh, it's common knowledge there's been something going on between those two. And also between him and most of the other queens at some point. Probably didn't want to give the game away to Linda's husband, in case it affected the divorce settlement.'

'Good Lord, I hadn't thought of that. How can he be so petty at a time like this, and even think about demanding his pesky flowers back? I'm wishing I'd never bought them now! Still, just in case he gets any ideas about pinching them at dead of night, I'm moving these round the back now, where I can keep an eye on them.'

'And I'm going back to sleep,' said Joshua. 'Good afternoon to you, my dear.'

With that he closed the window, and I went out to further festoon the apple tree. It was starting to look as if I was celebrating some ancient Druid rite. Then I settled down on the garden bench with a cup of iced tea and *The Bookseller* to try to regain my equilibrium, drifting in and out of sleep accompanied by nightmares of outsized birds and bees chasing me through a giant jungle of cottage garden flowers.

26

OCCUPATIONAL THERAPY

Back indoors alone, I found myself feeling in limbo, wishing the days away until the post-mortem results might come through. I decided I needed some occupational therapy to stop me going mad.

'What would Auntie May have done?' I asked myself. The answer came back loud and clear: she would write.

And not a moment too soon. Having joined the Wendlebury Writers, I would be asked to show them something that I'd written before long. The passage I'd rattled off for the Village Show competition wouldn't count, because entries were judged and displayed anonymously. Only the winners' names were revealed, and I was glad that I hadn't been publicly humiliated by how bad my piece was. I had carefully avoided that section of the tent, knowing how embarrassed I'd be to see my paltry words on display, even without my name attached to them.

I needed to create some credentials as a writer, and fast. This wasn't going to be easy, because in truth, as I'd hinted to Hector, I had never published anything beyond the odd adolescent poem in the school magazine. All I had to show for endless hours of pencil-chewing frustration was a collection of notepads in which I'd scrawled various fragments. My only reader had been Damian, who had poured scorn on them.

Yet I was nothing if not ambitious, sketching out plots for nail-biting thrillers, hysterical comic novels and tear-inducing chick lit that I hoped would eventually make me rich and famous. None of them were ever finished, either my enthusiasm or my confidence failing after a chapter or two. Even so, I'd lugged round a battered attaché case of manuscripts of dreadful short-stories and half-finished novels from one flat to the next, as I job-hopped around Europe. Used to travelling light, I had allowed myself the one luxury of hanging on to my old scribbles as my one self-indulgence.

Now I hauled the attaché case out from the cupboard under the stairs and hoisted it onto the sitting-room sofa. I turned the rusting wheels of the combination lock to my passcode and flung open the lid. Rooting among the half-filled notebooks, bought in the different countries I'd lived in while working abroad, I tried hard to find a piece of writing that I could pass off as a reasonable work in progress at the next Writers' meeting. I planned to get there early so the other members would find me scribbling away, looking as if I was used to spending my spare time writing in tearooms and bars, like J K Rowling and Ernest Hemingway. There were at least a couple of French exercise books in there that I might pass off as Parisian.

I don't know whether it was the vibes from Auntie May's cottage or my more mature outlook on life now that I'd become a householder instead of an itinerant, but I could find nothing that I would gladly share. Slapping the lid of the case shut, as if punishing it for defying my ambitions, and turning my back on it, I found myself drifting over to Auntie May's writing desk, hoping to absorb some of her talent by osmosis. Perching on her ancient bentwood chair, I pulled down the flap of her bureau. I reached out to touch the neat rows of stationery stowed in the little pigeonholes, waiting for May to write letters, articles and books that she now never would. It was the closest I'd get to being able to hold her papery old hand again.

Swinging my feet disconsolately under the desk, I banged them on the drawer beneath the flap. That reminded me I hadn't yet looked in the drawer. I wondered what I might find there. My imagination sprang into overdrive. Gold bullion? Emeralds? Blood diamonds gifted to her by a mysterious stranger on her last journey through Africa?

I tugged at the twin brass handles. The drawer was so stiff it rattled the brass stamp box on the top of the bureau. Bracing my foot against the wall between the spindly bent legs of the desk, I finally managed to wrench out the drawer. All that had been jamming it shut were great wads of letters, tied up in four distinct bundles. Decades of constant travelling had made Auntie May a frighteningly efficient packer.

Carefully, so as not to rip the paper, I pulled out the bundles and laid them on top of the flap.

The first set consisted of letters from my parents, written on pale blue Basildon Bond. These informed her of their latest news and were written every month or two, with extras following receipt of Christmas and birthday presents. They were tied together with a bit of silver string that might have originated on a festive box of violet creams, my parents' usual gift to May. I recognised my mother's dutiful approach to letter writing. Each time, she filled a regulation two sheets of paper on both sides, because one sheet would look like she didn't care. She'd run out of news by the end of the second.

The next bundle was, to my surprise, some tissue-thin carbon copies of the handwritten letters Auntie May had sent to me, one from every foreign trip she'd taken since I'd stopped visiting her in the summer. They were looped around with Post Office rubber bands, red faded to pink and starting to perish. Wise old Auntie May, she knew I'd lack the foresight to hang on to her letters. Or was it the entrepreneur in her that made her think they'd have potential value as a book? Perhaps it was from her that I'd inherited my head for business.

The third, tied up in pink ric-rac braid, was, to my embarrassment but also my delight, a raggedy package of mismatched stationery, much of it picture postcards from European cities. My own unmistakable hand came in an assortment of felt-tip, cheap biro, and even the occasional blunt pencil. On the one hand I dreaded reading them, fearing how awful and crass they might be, with patronising accounts of tourist traps that I hadn't the gumption to realise would be of little interest to such a seasoned traveller as May. But I was glad to see I'd always ended them with love and kisses, and was enormously grateful that she'd kept them. Though they'd be a much less likely candidate for a book than her letters, they at least provided a tangible souvenir of the last four years that I'd been frittering away, as if I had all the time in the world.

I wondered for a moment who the fourth package of letters could be from. She had no living relatives other than my parents and me, and had never married. Those letters looked very old. Perhaps they were from her parents or siblings. They'd all died before I was born, so I was intrigued.

The writing was old-fashioned in style, but the hand strong and firm, in the copperplate script taught as standard when May was a child. I stroked the paper, crisp with age and as brown as onion skin, and ran my forefinger gently along the red velvet ribbon holding them neatly together. A few threads came adrift, worn away by time. Afraid of untying the neat bow, in case it fell to bits entirely, I gently eased it down to the end of the bundle and slipped it off, still tied.

I peeled the first letter from the top of the pile and opened the single sheet flat. The steady, looping handwriting suggested a generous and open nature.

When I saw it began 'My darling May', I glanced at the signature before reading any more. 'Ever your loving Joshua' was followed with an extravagant row of kisses.

Open mouthed, I laid it down on the desk. This was not a friendly note between neighbours, one asking the other to feed the cat during their holiday, nor a missive between arch-enemies. I almost folded it up and stashed it back where I'd found it, not wishing to intrude on their secret relationship. Then I reconsidered.

Auntie May had left so many things ready in the knowledge that I'd come to live in her house eventually. Surely if she'd not wanted me to read these, she wouldn't have left them for me to find. I decided it would not count as prying if I read on. And the letters might contain vital evidence of Joshua's true character, giving clues as to whether he might have taken May's and Linda's lives, as well as his wife Edith's, and have designs on mine.

27

THREE LETTERS

I sat back in my chair and took a deep breath. This is what I read.

My darling May

I am so sorry that you decided to accept your publisher's offer of a contract to travel to Egypt to research and write that wretched book for them. When I say wretched, I don't mean the book will be wretched, because I know that in your meticulous, careful and thoughtful way, you will make a fine job of it. So fine, I fear, that they will offer you another contract, and another and another, taking you ever further away from where you belong – here with me in the village where we have both grown up.

I would not for a moment try to stop you from fulfilling your ambition. That is why I did not give you this letter before you went, or tell you of my feelings, but sent it on to your publisher's office in Cairo. By then, I am sure, you will be so taken up with your new surroundings and your new challenges that you may not care to read it, or even think of me, but there again I did not want you to depart thinking that I had let you go without a word because I no longer cared.

I of all people know what a fine mind and talent you have, and I cannot hope to offer you as glamorous or exciting a life if you stay here – nothing but the opportunity to look after my parents, now that yours have so sadly passed away. I know how much you suffered, almost as much as they did, during their final illnesses, and you have surely earned your chance for excitement abroad now.

Just know, my darling, that I shall still be here while you are abroad, and I will wait for you until you return, whenever that may be. Though of course I cannot wish for the departure of my own parents, I still cannot help but hope that one day, I shall be free to care only for you.

Please do not feel sorry for me, May, but send me a post-card now and again, will you, if you ever think of me on your travels? When you return, whenever you return, just tap on my door, and I will give you the best welcome that your heart could desire.

Ever yours,
Your loving Joshua.
xxxxx

So much for the feud. There was never any animosity, nor argument, nor clash. Quite the opposite, on his side at least.

I dared myself to pick the next letter off the pile. Auntie May, a meticulous record-keeper, had kept them neatly in chronological order.

My darling May,

I was so happy to receive your postcard from Cairo. Riding on a camel indeed! I hope it was in the company of someone who took good care of you, and that you avoid any hazards to your health.

Another six months, eh? I daresay it will go in no time for you, with your exotic travels and adventures. There must be so much to write up each night when you're not researching your book. You will sleep easily under the clear starry skies of the desert, so unlike the cloudy grey ones over the village now. All this rain is unhelpful to my mother's chest and my father's arthritis, and it becomes increasingly difficult to leave them each morning to go to work, or in the evening. I get no further than The Bluebird these days, but the new young lady behind the bar knows of my plight and feels sorry for me, slipping me extra pickled onions with my ploughman's of a lunchtime or secreting a penny bar of Cadbury's in my pocket as I take my leave. One must take one's comforts where one can, May! But I should not give you ideas.

Come home soon, May, and come home safe.

Ever your loving Joshua.

xxxxx

PS Do you still think of your cottage as home? I hope so.

Of course, who wouldn't keep reading? Though it made me want to run next door and throw my arms about poor abandoned Joshua's neck in pity.

My darling May,

So, Johannesburg now, eh? Another charming postcard. I had no idea what that great city might be like, except it seems as far away as anywhere in the world might be from here now. I suppose you will need that extra year for your analysis of South Africa, such a vast country. Wendlebury Barrow must seem so small by comparison – no wild game, no deserts or bush, just the common and the village pond, where you've as much chance of meeting a Martian as encountering an elephant.

It's little compensation that the house seems bigger since Mother and Father died. Barely had I got used to cooking for just two of us than Mother was taken as well. I tell myself it was for the best, as she grieved for Father so, after fifty-seven years of marriage.

It pains me to sit alone in the kitchen these days, May. I have taken to eating more of my meals at The Bluebird for company. At least now I have the leisure and the liberty to do more beyond the home, and tomorrow I am going to join the Village Show Committee. They are always shorthanded, and I am hoping to donate a trophy this year in memory of my beloved parents. I thought it should be for Best Jam in Show, my mother having always made such wonderful preserves from the fruit on my father's allotment. I hope you have not forgotten that night we lay concealed among the raspberry canes, gazing up at the stars, making plans for our future together?

I am fooling no-one, May, am I? Every time the trophy is presented, in my heart I shall be celebrating you.

Come home soon, May, and come home safe.

Ever your loving Joshua.

xxxxx

I sighed as I folded up the last letter and carefully reassembled the bundle. For the first time in my life, I felt ashamed of my aunt for responding to these earnest love letters with no more than a postcard. Then I blushed, ashamed of myself, for hadn't I responded to her long letters to me in just the same way?

Perhaps the messages on her cards had not been as shallow as mine. Maybe it was more than friendship that she'd renewed with Joshua after his wife's death. I wondered whether I'd ever find out.

But one thing I did know: this wasn't the correspondence between murderer and victim. How could I ever have suspected Joshua of anything so hideous against his beloved May? Or Edith, or Linda, or me, come to that?

A sudden recollection made me get up from my desk to visit the larder. There they were, just as I remembered: row upon row of May's home-made jam from last summer. All of them were raspberry. But it wasn't jam that I put on my toast for supper that night. I had my first taste of Joshua's honey.

28

DOCTOR'S VERDICT

On my way to work next morning, as I passed the village shop, Carol waved at me frantically through the window. Although I was not keen to see her until the post-mortem exonerated her from guilt, or at least I hoped so, it would have broken village etiquette to ignore her, so I popped in.

As I entered, she leaned over the counter to get closer to me, even though there was no-one else to overhear us in the shop.

'It wasn't natural causes. Linda Absolom died of fright.'

'Good Lord! How do you know?'

'Mrs Blake, who lives next door to the Absoloms, saw Mr Absolom coming home from the hospital. He's moved back in with the children, at least for the time being. So much for his other woman, poor soul. They haven't officially done the post-mortem yet, but when they got her into the ambulance, they said it looked like she'd died of fright. Rash all over, stuffocation, closing up of the throat. Horrible.'

I gasped, my own throat tightening out of sympathy. 'I didn't know fright could have that effect! That sounds more like an extreme allergic reaction, where your body goes into shock and starts shutting down. I've read about it on Facebook.'

'Oh, yes, not fright. It was shock. Prophylactic shock.'

I suppressed a snigger. Maybe Rex hadn't been thoughtful enough to buy hypoallergenic prophylactics.

'Oh dear, that's awful. I wonder what she was allergic to. Surely you can't die of hay fever?'

Carol looked horrified at the thought that the fragrance of her flowers might have been the kiss of death. 'Ooh no, I don't think so. She never had any antihistamines on her prescriptions. Only something for her heart, I think it was. Which would make more sense of the fright theory. Weak heart, fright, bam!'

She thumped her hand down on the wooden counter, making me jump.

'Should you really be telling me about her prescriptions? Doesn't that break patient confidentiality?'

'I'm only telling you. It's not as if I've taken that Hippopotamus oath – I'm not a doctor as such. I only hand over the prescription bags. Anyway, the prescription requests are always here for anyone to see, if they want to.'

Yes, and I don't think they should be, I thought, deciding to keep that to myself.

'She always looked healthy enough to me,' I said instead. 'Though cross. Usually cross whenever I saw her.'

'I think cross was her natural state,' said Carol. 'That's the way it is with some people. No wonder her marriage was in trouble. Those poor children.'

The shop doorbell jangled, and one of the mums I recognised from the school run strode in, making me realise that it was way past opening time at Hector's House.

'Sorry, Carol, I must fly. But thanks for telling me.'

That lets Carol off the hook, I considered as I marched swiftly up the High Street to Hector's House.

'Anaphylactic shock,' I announced to Hector as I swung open the bookshop door.

'And good morning to you too,' he replied, switching on his computer. 'Is that today's excuse for your lateness?'

I glanced quickly towards the tearoom to make sure we didn't have any customers yet. The morning rush had fallen away for the school holidays, but tended to pick up mid-morning when the mums took the children to the playpark nearby.

'It's what Linda died of. Carol just told me in the shop.'

'How does she know?'

'The Absoloms' next door neighbour spilled the beans.'

'Are you telling me Linda was fatally allergic to beans? That's a new one on me.'

I filled the water canister in the coffee machine and selected two capsules to make our morning coffee.

'No, but she was allergic to something. That's what killed her. We don't know what.'

'So natural causes after all?'

'Seems so.' I shouldn't have felt disappointed, but I did. 'But that doesn't make it any less mysterious. How can you die of an allergy when you're safely inside a costume, not doing anything? It doesn't make sense. And anyway, I've heard that you can't suddenly develop an extreme allergy. I looked it up once when I was worrying about eating too much peanut butter. It builds up slowly, so you have advance warning and can take avoiding action, like carrying an EpiPen.'

'Not much about Show Day makes sense sometimes,' said Hector. 'But if you like, there's the medical dictionary over there. If in doubt, consult a good book. That's my motto.'

At that moment, a group of three teenagers came in

demanding milkshakes. While I made them up, Hector flicked on BBC Radio 1 for their benefit.

Once they'd departed for the playpark with their shakes in takeaway cups, we resumed the conversation.

'Apparently certain medicines can increase your vulnerability to allergies, making future attacks more severe. I've just been looking it up in this book.' He tapped a huge family medical encyclopaedia that hogged a big space in the healthy living section.

'Carol told me Linda had a repeat prescription for heart medicine.'

'Good Lord, can't that woman keep any secrets? This is why I always make sure to collect my prescriptions from the chemist in town!' He smiled as he said this, reassuring me that he didn't have any dark medical secrets to hide. I grinned back.

'No, you're right there. She even told me on Show Day that you were being Homer because the Greeks invented Homer-sexuality!'

I laughed aloud then froze as I realised what I'd said. I suspected that was one secret he didn't want disclosed. To my relief, he laughed too, though looked slightly shamefaced.

'Ha, you rumbled me! I must confess, I did allow her to assume that I wasn't a ladies' man, when once at the village Halloween disco she seemed a little too eager to dance with me. Just for your information, Sophie, I am, by the way, very much a ladies' man. But please don't tell Carol.'

I gasped, and hoped he assumed it was with horror at her behaviour rather than with relief at his revelation.

'She is a bit of a Mrs Malaprop, isn't she?' I was pleased to have the chance to impress him with a literary reference, and hoped he didn't quiz me to see whether I knew where it came from. 'She also told me that Linda had died of fright. It took me a minute to work out she meant shock.'

He gave a sad smile.

'Well, whatever it was, it amounts to the same. The poor lady's still dead.'

Then the door swung open, setting the bell jangling. Enter stage right, Rex.

29

RECYCLING RITES

Not keen to see him after the previous day's encounter, I ran to the back of the shop and busied myself in the tearoom, washing up the milkshake blender. I returned to the front of the shop to speak to Hector only when Rex had gone.

'What did he want?' Conscious that my heart was pounding, I patted my chest to soothe it.

'Oh, for goodness' sake, don't tell me Rex makes your heart beat a little faster too? How does that man have that effect on so many ladies?'

I shook my head in vigorous denial and told him about Rex's little visit to me the day before. At the end, Hector smiled sympathetically.

'Don't worry, he didn't even mention that just now. He was only after a book he'd ordered. A biography of Laurence Olivier, would you believe? He really does give himself airs and graces. But it hasn't come yet. Can you drop the distributor an email to chase it up when you've got a moment, please?'

I nodded, relieved. Grabbing the duster from behind the

counter, I hoped the repetitive action of dusting the bookshelves might calm my nerves. Just then the doorbell jangled and in walked a delivery man with a parcel of about five books, judging from the size of it.

'Here you go, sweetheart, present for you,' he said, proffering the electronic tablet and stylus for my signature. 'All right, mate?' he added to Hector, trying to be friendly, but Hector was already bashing away at his keyboard, engrossed in whatever he was doing.

I laid down my duster, took the scissors from the pencil pot on the top of the counter, and slit the brown sticky tape that sealed the parcel. With perfect timing, it contained five books we'd ordered from the same publisher, one of which was Rex's Olivier biography. I waved it in front of Hector, who gave me a winning smile.

'I tell you what, to save us being subjected to an encore of Mr Stroppy's visit, could you run down the road and pop it through his letter box? He paid for it when he placed the order, so there's no need to see him. Just stick it in a jiffy bag first to keep it pristine. Then when you get back, you could put our paper recycling out for collection.'

Still basking in the implications of Hector's confession, I trotted back to the stockroom and pulled down an old white padded envelope from the top shelf where we stored them for re-use. I was so wrapped up in romantic speculation about Hector that I didn't notice I'd dislodged a large fat spider until it fell into my hair, waving it legs ferociously. Hector came running at my screams, then braked to a halt in the doorway when he saw my unexpected attacker.

'Oh, for goodness' sake, I thought for a minute you were being attacked by a crazed murderer, or at least had a major health and safety issue.' Carefully, with apparently more thought for the spider's well-being than mine, he caught it up in his cupped hands and released it through the open window. Abashed by my squeamishness, I dashed off to deliver Rex's book without demur.

* * *

Rex's house, or rather Dido's, was about halfway between the village shop and Hector's House. I confess I'd sped up as I'd walked to work that morning, really not wanting to encounter the man himself after our disagreement the day before. His front path was overflowing with butterfly lavender in full fragrant bloom. I couldn't help treading on a few stalks as I ran up the path, so I hoped he wasn't watching me, if he was still at home.

Once I'd deposited his book through the front door, I ran back down the path as fast as I could. Unfortunately, I stumbled as I jumped down the step onto the pavement, and almost fell flat on my face, my fall cushioned only by Rex's recycling boxes, already put out for collection. Both of them tipped over, and the papers that had been held by a brick were soon flying down the street, with me rushing after them. Luckily the breeze was blowing in the direction of Hector's House, so once I'd turned the boxes the right way up and replaced the brick, I was able to gather up any stray bits of paper as I headed back to the shop, stuffing them in my pockets rather than doubling back to put them in Rex's box. The less time I spent outside Rex's house, the better.

Hector was busy on the phone when I got back, and pointed at the cardboard wrapper from the books to remind me what I was meant to do next. I hauled the big box of cardboard from the storeroom on to the pavement. Only when I returned for the box of paper did I remember my pockets full of Rex's scraps.

On the run from his house, I'd screwed up his paper scraps anxiously. In the interests of neatness, I flattened them out on the counter now, intending to add them to our own neat recycling box, burying them beneath a pile of old computer printouts so that there'd be no chance of Rex spotting them if he happened to walk by. Most of them were supermarket or petrol receipts, but to my horror there was a larger sheet of printer paper bearing a list of familiar phrases, each one allocated against the name of a famous writer.

It was Rex's checklist for the notes he'd planted on the Wendlebury Writers' float.

'My goodness, look at this, Hector!' I slammed my hand down on the counter for emphasis. 'It was Rex who pulled those pranks. What an awful man! Pretending to be all charming to the ladies, then doing a thing like that! Why would he be so unkind?'

Hector let out a low whistle. 'Just to put you off your stride, maybe? He's very competitive. Weak ego, I reckon. Now that he hasn't got his lovely assistants from his conjuring days to big him up, maybe making everyone else feel small makes him feel better.'

I nodded. 'He did seem keen to beat everyone else on the coconut shy. How pathetic. Still, I don't think he ought to be allowed to get away with it.'

As a sudden thought struck me, I clapped my hand over my mouth. 'My God, I've just remembered something that proves he set up the Suffragettes too. I saw him drop a little key in the beer tent. At the time I thought it was for his codpiece.' Hector guffawed. 'But now I realise it must have been for the Suffragettes' padlock. What a complete git.'

'So, what are you going to do about it, Wonder Woman? Take away his coconuts?'

'No. But I'll give him a piece of my mind. Once I've thought of exactly what to say, that is.'

'Good luck with that. Just don't do anything silly. You don't want him setting his white rabbit on you. You never know.' He smiled and winked. 'Stay safe, Sophie.'

30

WRITERS' RIGHTS

On my way home, I had to drop another book into the pub: a cookery book which Donald the publican had ordered as a birthday present for his wife. I was the only customer there besides the inevitable Billy who was propping up the bar.

'So, girlie, what do you reckon on this business with Mrs Absolom?' he quizzed me as I waited for Donald to emerge from the back room. 'I reckon it was that Rex what done it.'

'Really? You think she was allergic to Rex? Now there's a theory I can relate to. I don't know what anyone sees in him.' All afternoon I'd been half expecting Rex to come barging into the shop to shout at me for damaging his lavender.

'No, but I reckon that varmint was up to something,' said Billy. 'I heard the two of them having a humdinger of a row a few days before. She was giving him a hard time about the costumes.'

'I can't think why. The costumes were beautiful. Carol's wasted in that shop, you know. She's very talented, creatively speaking. She could be a professional costume designer.'

Billy took a long slurp from his pint of bitter and scratched his head.

'It wasn't so much the dresses as the flowers she was fussed about. Didn't like the thought of having real flowers about her person. I could understand it if it was Rex wanting fake ones, like he must have used in his magic act. But it's a funny sort of a woman what don't like real flowers, if you asks me.'

I nodded. 'I know, and the flowers Carol did were beautiful. I bought them at the auction afterwards. They're lovely, though a bit highly scented for indoors. They attracted loads of butterflies when I hung them up in my garden.'

'She weren't natural, if you ask me,' went on Billy. 'Not a normal woman, that Linda Absolom.'

'What, you mean she found you attractive?' Donald quipped as he appeared behind the bar, looking pleased with himself for getting one over on Billy.

It was time for a hasty exit, before the conversation descended any lower.

* * *

The Wendlebury Writers were due to meet next evening at Hector's House. Before leaving work at the end of the afternoon, I consulted Hector further about Rex.

'I'd hate to get it wrong in front of all the other writers,' I told him. 'I think maybe I'll go down and confront him about it now. Then I will make him come to the Writers' meeting this evening and apologise to them all. That'll teach him.'

Hector raised his eyebrows. 'You sure you know what you're doing?'

'Yep, I shall strike while the iron's hot. I'll go in while I'm still feeling invincible.'

I wasn't, but I thought if I said I was, I might.

'Okay, if you must. Have you got your shop key with you, to

get back in if I've gone by the time you come back for the meeting?'

I patted my pocket. 'It's in here with the evidence. Wish me luck.'

'Good luck,' he said solemnly as he powered down his computer.

Once I got outside the door, I felt my courage ebbing away, so I made myself march smartly up to Rex's door and rap really hard with the knocker. I thought a noisy entrance might have the same effect as ancient warriors banging their shields with their swords to frighten the enemy.

To my surprise, Rex was all oily charm when he came to the door. Well, he was an actor.

'To what do I owe the pleasure?' I wondered whether he had company that he was trying to impress, or whether Dido was home during the week for once. I tried to peer around him to see who else was there, but couldn't spot anyone.

Here's where I'd been especially clever. From within my shoulder-bag, I produced one of the posies that I'd concealed there all day. Not so clever was that I'd forgotten that at its centre was a ball of green florists' sponge, soaked in water, which had now drenched the inside of the bag.

'I brought you one of these as a peace offering,' I began, 'provided that you can spare me a moment for a little chat.'

To be honest, I was glad to see the back of this one, because it had been Anne Boleyn's. I was sure Rex wouldn't have remembered which was which, and it gave me positive pleasure to pass this one off on to him.

Rex flashed me his most winning smile and stood back to allow me to cross the threshold. He probably thought I wanted to talk to him about the script.

'Why not have a drink while you're here?' he suggested. 'I was just about to have a little G and T myself.'

He raised the full crystal tumbler that was in his hand and beckoned me to follow him through to his kitchen. On the worktop lay a marble chopping board and knife with half a lemon cut side down. He took another tumbler from a cupboard and cut some wafer-thin lemon slices so easily that the knife must have been very sharp indeed. Feeling a little weak at the knees, I placed the damp floral ball on his draining board and sat down at his kitchen table. After drying my hands on my skirt, I dug into my pockets to reassure myself that the tell-tale sheet of paper was still there.

He set the nearly empty gin bottle on the counter with a thud. I suspected this was not his first drink of the day. He rummaged in the fridge for the tonic, plucked some ice cubes from the freezer, and topped the glass with a sliver of lemon before pressing it into my hand. Then he raised a toast, chinking his glass against mine with an intimate leer.

'So, have you come to talk to me about your ideas for your play script? We'll need to start rehearsing in January, so sight of the script in October would be good, to allow for rewriting.'

I played him along for a little while. 'Of course. Although I expect you'll be focusing on your autumn show till it's over in November.' He nodded. 'Which I suppose will be extra hard now that you have to recruit another Anne Boleyn.'

He looked puzzled, as if he didn't know which way I was going with this. Neither did I.

'Were you thinking of auditioning, then?' he queried. 'I'm sure you'd be perfect for the part.'

This was a turn-up for the books (drat that Wendlebury Writers' cliché box!). I'd spent the last four years resenting my boyfriend for not offering me a speaking part in one of his plays, and here was my arch enemy offering me one on a plate. I jumped at the chance.

'Really?' Then I pulled myself together, remembering what I'd come for. I was supposed to be calling the shots here. 'But first, I need to talk to you about something that happened on Show Day. You see, I think you pulled a little trick there that no-one else but me has rumbled yet. But I need to nip it in the bud. Rex, I know what you did, and I can't allow you to pull that same stunt again. It was far too upsetting for us all.'

The buzzing of a large bee interrupted my train of thought. It flew in through the open kitchen window and landed on the floral ball. Rex got up and slammed the window shut, with the bee still on the inside.

You're not as bright as you think, I admonished him in my head. You should have chased the bee out first. Having the large furry bee buzzing around just a few feet away made me a little more anxious, but at least it wasn't a spider.

The bee stopped buzzing as it set about gathering some pollen from within a large pink scabious at the centre of the floral ball. Almost immediately it set off again, this time attracted by the lemon in my drink, just as I was raising the glass to my lips. Thinking it was about to fly right inside my mouth, I let out a piercing scream and shot out of my seat, knocking my chair over in the process. It fell to the floor with a great clatter. I couldn't take my eyes off the enormous beast.

'So, you're another one not keen on bees.' I wondered if Rex was now trying to big himself up as the great defender of feeble women from fierce insects. I refused to let him have the upper hand.

'Bees, schmees,' I surprised myself by saying. 'I've rumbled you, Rex, and I want you to promise never to do such a dreadful thing again.' I felt in my pocket for his list of pranks and waved it as proof. 'I demand a public apology.'

It was Rex's turn to look rattled. 'An apology? To whom? And what good would that do?'

'I know why you did it, you know.' The bee started buzzing again, and I drew back as far as I could on to my seat.

'You bloody little bitch!' He seized the lemon knife, a look of sheer panic on his face. So much for his acting ability. But then he grabbed me by the shoulder and spun me round so that I had my back to him. With one arm he pinned me to his chest while with the other he held the knife against my throat. I lost my grip on the sheet of paper, which fluttered down to the floor unseen, and let out another piercing scream.

'For God's sake, no!'

'Who have you told?'

I thought fast. 'Hector. Only Hector. Though I'll tell the Wendlebury Writers at the meeting tonight. And the WI!'

I had never felt so defiant, and in that moment I realised I would never let myself be bullied or bossed about by a man again, even if he had a knife in his hand.

'Oh, so they can write their pretty poems about it? Death of an actress? Ode to a bee?'

'Ode to a bee? What do you mean? I'm talking about all those awful pranks you played on us on our float, and the Suffragettes, just to give yourself a chance of winning the cup for your float. And you still didn't win it anyway, so there!'

'And what makes you think you'll be at the Wendlebury Writers meeting anyway? You're not going anywhere with that blabbing mouth of yours.'

He set the point of the knife closer to my throat. I felt a pinprick piercing of my skin, just as I heard the back door being flung open. Thankfully, no-one ever keeps their doors locked when they're at home in the village.

'Drop it, Rex,' a familiar voice said behind us. Suddenly I was free, and in a flash Hector had Rex in a headlock, doubled up on the kitchen table. 'What were you going to do, saw her in half?'

Rex spluttered, inarticulate.

'So it was all done with bees, was it?' Hector continued. 'And you damn near got away with it, too. I'm still not sure how you persuaded the bees to sting Linda, but I'm pretty sure it was bees that triggered her fatal allergic reaction. What a terrible way to go, dying in front of everyone, concealed in plain sight, trapped inside that hideous costume. How long had you known she was allergic to bees, Rex? I suspect she'd tried to keep it secret since she lived here, but did you witness her suffering from bee stings in her younger days, when she was working for you? Did you know that with every attack, the reaction gets more severe? That the heart drugs she'd recently started taking increased the risk? Now I know why she kept ordering different books about bees, though never a beekeeper herself.'

Released from Rex's grip, I recovered my breath. 'That must be why she'd been pestering Carol to stock Joshua's honey in the shop, to inoculate herself against the village bees. She probably didn't dare go round to Joshua's house to ask for it, in case she encountered bees from the hives in his garden. The poor woman must have been terrified.'

How ironic that the intervention of a randomly visiting bee had been the catalyst for my rescue. If I hadn't screamed when it came near me, maybe Hector would never have come running. Maybe the bee was the ghost of Linda Absolom coming back to get her revenge. Maybe she hadn't disliked me as much as I'd thought.

If the bee was Linda, she was very forgiving, because instead of stinging Rex, it flew straight out of the back door the minute it was opened again by Rex's next-door-neighbour, letting himself in to see what all the noise was about. His intervention was clearly out of curiosity rather than concern for Rex's well-being.

'What's this old bugger been up to now?' he asked brightly, crossing over to help Hector keep Rex pinned to the table. 'Sophie, I think you'd better run out and give our Bobby a shout.'

'Wouldn't it be better to dial 999?'

'No, Bob lives the other side from me. He's in the back garden watering his dahlias. Tell him to get himself down here quick, and he can take charge.'

* * *

Ten minutes later, I was on the outside of a glass of brandy in the pub, with Hector's arm protectively about me. I'd gone right off gin.

'Had a change of heart, girlie?' called Billy from his habitual bar stool. 'Not meeting your writing chums at Hector's House after all? It must be bad if not even Hector wants to be there.'

I was shaking too much to reply.

'How did you magically appear in Rex's kitchen?' I asked Hector, gripping his arm as if to reassure myself that he was real. 'I thought he was the conjuror, not you.'

'Easy. I was just setting the burglar alarm at the shop when I heard you scream. I'd have known it anywhere. Don't forget, I heard you being mugged by that spider in the stockroom yesterday. I thought perhaps it had followed you to Rex's.'

I squeezed his arm tighter in gratitude.

'So it was a bee sting all along. Who'd have thought it?' Hector continued. 'Poor Linda, not a very dignified way to go. But

I'm wondering why she didn't carry an EpiPen, if she had a bad allergy to bee stings?'

Someone had called the doctor from across the road to come and see that I was all right. I hadn't yet registered with him as his patient, but he didn't mind being called on in a crisis. It gave him a fast track into local gossip.

'Couldn't happen,' he said, 'unless there was either a huge swarm or reduced immunity.'

'Heart medicine?' suggested Hector. 'Apparently she had tablets prescribed for her heart.'

The doctor looked grim. 'Beta blockers. It's a possibility. The patient could pass out at the first impact, but the application of an EpiPen followed by emergency treatment could have saved her. On the other hand, if it happened when she was on her own, and she was stung repeatedly before anyone could discover her, it could be too late. Surely she was in public view on a float on Show Day?'

'Yes, but enveloped inside a costume that concealed her face and body. Her reaction would have been invisible. If she had been able to cry out for help before she lost consciousness, the noise of the band and the crowds would have drowned her out. Of course, we would have noticed if she'd keeled over, but she was wired to the safety rail round the trailer to stop her falling off it where she knelt before the chopping block. Awaiting her execution. Oh my goodness.'

Hector shuddered and lapsed into silence.

The doctor took over. 'I suspect she would have died before you'd even reached the showground. But best leave it to the experts now. The post-mortem will reveal all, I'm sure. But what's puzzling me now is how did the bees get inside the dress? There's still no real evidence to suggest anything other than natural causes, apart from Rex having a bit of brainstorm and threatening young Sophie here.'

'And why those stupid pranks?' I queried.

'Distraction techniques, I reckon. Diverting attention away from the Players' float will have given him longer to introduce the bees to Linda's costume without anyone noticing. He knew from the numbers given out the night before the Show which groups' floats would be either side of his. That's how he was able to target your writer friends so precisely. But why go to all that trouble? That's what I'd like to know now.'

'The truth will out,' called Billy. 'There's no smoke without fire.'

If he'd been at the Wendlebury Writers' meeting, that would have cost him 20p.

31

BEWARE OF THE WARDROBE

As it turned out, Billy was right. A couple of days later, when Carol finally got round to hanging all the Tudor costumes up in the drama wardrobe at the back of the Village Hall, a small plastic snack box dropped out of Henry VIII's codpiece. Through its clear lid, she could see little dark shapes and assumed it was a sustaining handful of nuts and raisins, to keep Rex's energy levels up on Show Day. She flipped the lid off, planning to eat a raisin or two, when she realised these weren't dried fruit, but the dead bodies of plump, fuzzy bees.

She immediately ran from the Hall to Bobby's house with the box of bees in her hand and pounded on the door, crying, 'Officer, arrest these bees!'

Bob took it in good heart. 'No, they can't be the culprits,' he told her, resealing the box and placing it inside a plastic bag for fingerprinting later. 'They will have been inside the dress. I would say these were the culprits' understudies – reinforcements in case the first batch didn't do the trick. But let's take a look at Linda's dress.'

He followed Carol over to the Hall. Together they gathered up the thick velvet folds of Anne Boleyn's costume and shook it out onto the parquet flooring. Sure enough, a dozen or more bees dropped out. With a pair of tweezers borrowed from the Village Hall first aid box, Bob added them to the plastic bag. He also took away the dress 'for questioning', as Carol confided in me the next day.

'But how could Rex have forced quantities of bees into Linda's dress?' I asked Hector in the bookshop later.

'Don't forget he was a conjuror by trade,' said Hector. 'Sleight of hand may not have been easy with a fistful of bees, but I'm sure, drawing on his old conjuring skills, he could have done it, especially when the folk on the floats were otherwise preoccupied – the Wendlebury Players with striking poses, the Suffragettes chained into place facing the other way, and you Wendlebury Writers getting aereated by the stupid notes he'd secreted on to your persons. If I were not such a subtle type, I might even say you all had a bee in your collective bonnet about them.'

'Next Show Day, I think I'll stay at home quietly with a good book,' I told him.

* * *

It wasn't till I got home and was sitting on my back garden bench, watching the remaining five posies blowing gently in the breeze under the apple tree, that I remembered I had another question as yet unanswered. Joshua was hoeing beneath his runner beans, whistling quietly. I got up and walked down to lean over the wall.

'Joshua,' I called. 'Can I ask you something?'

'And good evening to you too, my dear,' he smiled. 'Yes, fire away.'

'So we think it's pretty clear now that poor Linda died from a fatal reaction to multiple bee stings, to which she was particularly sensitive due to the heart medication that she was on.'

'Ah, that would explain why she was so keen to have some of my honey. How sad that she was too frightened to come to my door to ask for some. If only I'd known, I'd gladly have given her a jar with my compliments.'

I frowned. 'That's tragic. But what we still don't know is why would Rex set her up for such an awful thing?'

He leaned on his hoe thoughtfully. 'Any number of reasons may come out in court. Or if the Lord prefers, perhaps we'll never know.'

32

UNMASKED

The evidence did indeed come out at the trial, many months later. The local paper, the *Weekly Slate*, devoted a full page to reporting from the court, week by week, with a front page splash and double page spread inside when the guilty verdict was finally announced.

The day that paper came out, Carol beckoned me into the shop on my way to work. Although we'd both been called in as witnesses, and the village grapevine, fuelled by social media, had circulated facts and fiction about the trial as it took place, we'd been looking forward to seeing the eventual report in the newspaper to draw a line under the whole unpleasant business.

As the bell jangled me into the shop, Carol was spreading out several copies of the paper on the counter, to show off the five pages of articles at a glance. I leaned over to have a good look.

'I'm glad Mr Absolom got their children away from the village before this came out. It wouldn't have done any of them any good to read about what Rex claimed were the mitigating circumstances. I wonder how her poor husband must have felt when he realised Linda hadn't been having an affair with Rex after all. What a tragic waste.'

Carol pointed to a photo of Linda and Rex together in their younger days. 'I never knew she was a contortionist. Of course, Rex had told us about his previous career as a magician, but he'd kept it quiet about his other reasons for being famous.' She tapped her nose knowingly. 'Spite of hand, you see. Doesn't do any good to mess with nature.'

I bought a copy of the paper for myself, plus one to put in the tearoom, where I knew it would be in demand. I had a quick read of the main article on my walk from the shop, but didn't want to make myself even later by reading the full reports inside.

* * *

Hector claimed first dibs on the paper before the school-run mums arrived.

'So the old bugger was interfering with his lovely assistants, eh?' He pored over the black and white photos of the young Rex performing a magic show in Bognor. 'Blimey, I wouldn't have recognised Linda Macarthur as our Linda Absolom. She was quite a beauty before she had the budget for Botox.'

'It seems she was the one who blew the whistle on him and got him sacked, although no-one had the sense to press charges. I think it would be harder for him to escape unscathed from something like that today. Let's just hope he doesn't also have escapology among his party tricks.'

Hector read on. 'At least he was cast out of the Magic Circle for bringing it into disrepute. You'd think they'd just make him vanish.'

He turned over to see the detailed biography of both parties that was printed on the next page, Linda's in the form of a glowing obituary, Rex's as the world's worst CV. The report included a big graphic demonstrating when Linda's and Rex's lives had crossed at various times on the seaside theatre circuit, and later when Rex had moved to Wendlebury Barrow to take up the latest in a series of high school teaching posts, falling back on his first career as a drama teacher. All along, he'd fed his love of the spotlight by starring in or directing local amateur drama companies, each of which was listed by name.

'Do you reckon they were all as bad as the Wendlebury Players?' Hector wondered aloud, not without a certain pride.

'He must have got a shock when he pitched up to join as director and found Linda Macarthur waiting to audition,' I considered. 'I suppose it's a credit to their acting skills that they got through two whole productions without giving the game away.'

'But no surprise. Rex obviously had nothing to gain by airing his sordid past. And Linda was smart about it. She realised she could use his guilty secret to her advantage. I always wondered why he cast her in leading parts when she was such a dreadful actress. Now we know. It's just a shame everyone assumed they were having an affair, not least her husband.'

'Maybe that's what drove him into the arms of another woman?' I suggested.

Hector looked up at me over the top of the paper. 'You old romantic, you!'

I went round to stand behind him to look at the pictures on the double-page spread. The large photo above the tribute to Linda showed her with her ex-husband in happier times.

'If he was her ex-husband, does that make him an ex-widower?' I queried, before going over to the tearoom to put out today's cake delivery.

'I don't know, but his ex-wife was certainly an ex-tortionist.'

I laughed. 'So that's what Carol meant this morning. Not a contortionist.'

Hector grinned. 'Now that could have made for a whole different story.'

Seeing the parents and children heading up the High Street towards the school, I left Hector to it and went over to fill the kettle and the water reservoir of the coffee machine.

'I'd have had more sympathy for Linda if she hadn't got greedy about it, and added financial blackmail to her list of charms.'

'Tempting, though, when she knew Rex's girlfriend was loaded. Dido's quite high up in some City finance firm, you know. Linda's lavish lifestyle took a downturn when her husband moved out to be with his new woman. It wasn't rocket science to seek withdrawals from the Bank of Rex in return for not spilling the beans to Dido.'

'Why didn't Rex go to the police about her threats?'

Hector raised his eyebrows. 'Do you really need to ask? That would have required a confession of his sordid past, so he'd have lost Dido one way or another – and his own subsidised lifestyle. His teacher's salary must have been pin-money in their house. Dido owned the house long before they were an item. No, for someone like Rex, with an inflated sense of his own abilities, it was much easier to take the law into his own hands, especially when he remembered Linda's potentially fatal bee allergy. When he spotted her prescription request for beta blockers in the shop, he must have done his research and found out, as it explains in the paper, that they can make future attacks more severe.'

'Carol thinks they're called beetle blockers,' I remembered. 'Bee blockers would have been more useful. Did I tell you, Billy heard Rex and Linda having a row in the pub because Linda wanted fake flowers on their float? Rex was refusing point blank, saying it was against the spirit of a horticultural show, but now it seems Rex had more sinister reasons. He made Carol use really strongly perfumed flowers too, the sort that Auntie May used to say attracted bees.'

'So it seems Rex had the makings of a perfect murder. If only he could introduce the bees without anyone seeing, her death would be attributed to natural causes. Turning a loaded bee on his victim would be easier to conceal than a loaded gun. She must have blacked out when the first sting entered her blood-stream. Subsequent stings would seal her fate in silence, in her personal Room 101 hell. Room 101, Sophie? I take it you've read George Orwell's *1984*?'

I sighed. 'I know it's from a book, not the television programme. I'm not a complete ignoramus.'

Predictably Hector got up from his seat to fetch a copy from the classics section and dropped it on the tearoom counter for me. He then folded back the paper to read out a funny sketch that the reporter had written of Rex using all his dramatic powers in court to portray the wronged victim. Rex had pinned the blame on a passing swarm of bees, possibly from a local hive kept by one Joshua Hampton.

'What? How dare he accuse Joshua! How could he possibly expect to pin a murder on that lovely old gentleman?' I cried, then blushed as I remembered that not long ago, I'd had him down as a ruthless poisoner of old ladies.

Hector carried on reading. 'When the prosecution pressed him, he could not say why they had found Linda's personal scent more appealing than the nearby marquee packed with exhibition standard flowers, cakes, fruit and vegetables.'

I laughed. 'I wish I'd been a fly on the wall in that courtroom.'

'Not a bee?'

I shook my head. 'I've gone right off bees. I should think Carol has too. Speaking of Carol, I'm glad they've done a special box story there about how her evidence helped convict him. That'll make her feel better after being unwittingly duped into baiting his bee trap and stitching Linda into her costume to await her fate.'

'Well, I just hope everyone reads the full report. Then they'll accept that no-one was to blame but Rex and Linda themselves.' Hector closed the paper, folding it in half, before chucking it onto the nearest tearoom table. 'And I've no doubt they will. Our copy will be in shreds by the time the school mums have finished with it.'

Fortunately Hector was right. Even so, as Dinah had predicted, the next Show Committee meeting accepted a proposal from the Wendlebury Players to name a new trophy the Linda Absolom Cup for Best Honey in Show. Only Billy had the gall to say what everyone else was thinking: that this whole business should draw bumper crowds from miles around to next year's Village Show. I was looking forward to it already.

33

FULL CIRCLE

Of course, we had to wait many months for the case to come to court and for justice to be done. Meanwhile, the village had returned to its normal routine after the excitement of Show Day. The start of the new school year brought the return of my pupils to the bookshop, and it felt as if all the excitement of summer was over.

A postcard arrived from my parents who were holidaying in the Canary Islands, courtesy of Auntie May's royalties. It turned out she'd left them to my dad as her next of kin.

Realising I'd missed out on a summer holiday this year, I decided to indulge in a bit of armchair travel instead. It was about time I read some of Auntie May's books. One evening after work, I took down from the bedroom bookshelf her account of her travels in the Outer Hebrides. Characteristically, May didn't visit in the region's brief summer to bask in twenty-four hour daylight and jewel-coloured seas and skies. Instead, in midwinter, she rented a remote blackhouse, experiencing raw, wild weather and short, sodden days. Her scheduled week spilled over into a fortnight, thanks to seas too rough to permit ferry crossings. By the time she was able to leave, she had fallen in love with the place, returning to use it as a writing retreat when pressed by a stiff deadline.

Despite autumnal sunshine fading outside my open bedroom window, and heady wafts of night-scented stock drifting up through the warm evening air, her opening page immediately transported me to a Hebridean island in winter, overwriting the English summer garden scents with the choking fug of peat smoke. I turned the page, reaching with my other hand for the mug of cocoa on my nightstand, and out of the corner of my eye saw a slip of brown and white paper flutter from between the pages. Setting my cocoa down again to investigate, I found myself looking at a Bank of Scotland note with a face value of £100.

I did a double-take. There was something odd about this book. I realised for the first time that it looked distorted, with the pages thicker than the spine was designed to accommodate. It reminded me of a paperback that had been dropped in the bath, making the body of the book expand, crinkly paged, while the binding remained the same size.

On a whim, I held the book by the spine and gently shook it. Out fluttered a confetti of banknotes, most of them green, but some blue and the odd one pink. Gathering them together on top of the counterpane, I sorted them by colour then totted up the total: £1,245, including the £100 that I'd found after the first page.

At last I understood Auntie May's message: 'There's money in books'. Tucked inside the first editions of each of her books on the special shelf by her bed was a secret stash of cash, concealed where only I'd be likely to find it once I'd moved into her cottage.

I counted twenty-seven books on the shelf. Getting up, I pulled down all of her first editions and set them gently on the bed. I picked each one up in turn and held it, spine uppermost, and pulled the covers back to open the pages. Each time, a pile of banknotes, in various currencies, fluttered out onto the patch-work quilt. I didn't need to count them to be able to make an accurate guess that there were over ten thousand pounds.

Then another awful thought occurred to me. What if I hadn't bothered to read the books but had shipped them wholesale to a charity shop, or put them on eBay? That would have served me right.

From the look in Joshua's eye earlier that evening, I suspected that he knew of her plan. When I'd pressed him, he revealed she'd been using this system for years, slipping money in books to Carol, for example, as a surreptitious gift to help lighten her difficult load of nursing her dying mother. Fortunately, May must have stashed her cash away relatively recently, because the foreign money was all in Euros or dollars of various countries, and the sterling was the latest design.

For a moment, I wondered whether Auntie May hadn't meant for me to write at all, just to find the money that she'd hidden in *her* books to reward me for continuing to read them after she'd gone. But no, she had spent the last fifteen years giving me note-books and pens and encouragement. And there was her last message of all, written in the little green Moleskine book that still lay, as blank as she'd left it, on my nightstand: 'Live a life worth writing down. Then write it down.'

I gathered up the money, stashed it all into one of her Moroccan leather purses, and put it under my pillow for safe-keeping. I realised I should count it properly and get it to the bank for safekeeping, and then I should tell my dad, who was sorting out the legal stuff to do with her will and probate. But that could wait. I knew exactly what I needed to do next.

I picked up her pen, opened the green Moleskine notebook, and began to write. I was on my way.

EPILOGUE
HOMERIC JUSTICE

I couldn't wait to get to work next day to tell Hector about my good fortune.

'So you see, I don't need this job any more, and you don't have to pay me, and your shop will stay in business.'

Hector looked both bewildered and a little sad. 'Pardon?'

'I know you only took me on because you felt indebted to my aunt, rather than because you needed me or could afford an extra member of staff. Now you're off the hook. I'll be able to buy a car and drive beyond the village to get a job. Once I've learned to drive, anyway.'

Hector minimised whatever he was typing on his computer and sat back on the stool, arms folded across his chest.

'First of all, I do need an extra pair of hands in the shop, and if I hadn't appointed you, it would have been one of the many other applicants that you detected in the recycling box, if you cast your mind back.

'Secondly, I can afford your wages, thank you very much. Thanks to my fine business acumen and skilful diversification, my shop is profitable.'

'I'm sorry, Hector, I find it hard to believe that my presence in the shop has brought in so much more business that you can justify my wages, even with the sponsorship you get from Literally Gifted and the income from my teaching books.'

'No, you silly girl, what you've done is given me back my time, which I've been using very fruitfully on the computer, in case you haven't noticed.'

'But how has that helped? I mean, what can you have been doing on it to make so much money? Playing the stock market? Oh no, don't tell me you're a gambling addict!'

How could I have been so stupid not to have noticed? No wonder he often looked so emotional when plugging away at the computer, and could be irritable if interrupted by a customer or a phone call.

He sat quietly for a moment, and I fiddled nervously with the pink string bracelet that Jemima had given me at our last lesson. Then he pointed over to the fiction display in the window.

'Please bring me a book by the author who is our top fiction seller,' he instructed me.

That was easy. I plucked Hermione Minty's latest blockbuster, *Touched by Love*, out of the window and set it down on the counter in front of him.

'Now tell me her name.'

'Hermione Minty.'

'Anything strike you as familiar about Hermione Minty?'

I stared at the book for a clue, turned it over to scan the blurb on the back, then opened the cover to read the sparse author bio within.

'Hermione Minty enjoys a private life in a charming English village, where she has many strings to her bow.'

I clicked at once.

'She's a violinist? She lives here in the village?'

'Look at the initials.'

As I examined the book again, he deftly set a poignant violin solo playing on the shop's sound system. When I looked up, I clocked his enormous, self-satisfied grin, like someone who's just won a lengthy game of charades.

'You mean, you're Hermione Minty?'

'Yes. Would you like my autograph? Mind you, I can charge an extra fiver for signed copies of my books on eBay. That pays the shop's electricity bill, for starters.'

'You've had me fooled. Ever thought you should take over from Rex at the Wendlebury Players? You're certainly the better actor. You could win prizes for it.'

Hector nodded appreciatively, then reached into his bag to produce a large Manilla envelope, addressed to me care of the shop, and a small piece of thin red cardboard.

'By the way, speaking of prizes, you've won something. Two things, in fact.'

'Me? How? I haven't entered any competitions lately.'

'Oh, but you have. Firstly, you don't seem to have noticed that your entry in the new nature writing competition class at the Village Show won first prize: the princely sum of £2.50 and a certificate the size of a postcard. I'm sure you won't let it change your life.'

'How lovely! I'm an award-winning writer at last!' I hugged the certificate proudly to my chest and wondered where I'd hang it once it was framed. Then a dreadful thought occurred to me. 'Mine wasn't the only entry, was it?'

I'd noticed several fruit and vegetable classes in the Show had fewer than three submissions, though first, second and third prizes were set aside for each one. In some cases, a solitary entry had been awarded third prize, indicating that it wasn't worthy of first or second, even without competition.

Hector reassured me. 'There were at least a dozen, and I read them all. Most of the others were straight descriptions, smacking of school essays – two hundred and fifty words on a squirrel, or whatever. But yours had heart. Nature was only a jumping-off point for a deeper and more far-reaching piece about the human condition.

'Really?' I said lightly. 'And there was me thinking I'd just written about Auntie May's garden.'

He looked at me reproachfully. 'No, it was lovely, demonstrating the inextricable relationship between the garden, your aunt and you. It was very touching, very individual – and very you.'

His kind words and his warm gaze upon me now were worth so much more than £2.50.

'I still can't believe I won a prize for my writing! I can't wait to tell Damian.'

Hector raised his eyebrows. 'Don't tell me you two are getting back together? I would have thought you'd had enough of actors.'

I laughed. 'God, no! I just want to prove to him that at least someone thinks my writing is worthwhile. He was always so dismissive of it. It was very hurtful.'

Hector tutted. 'I don't know why you value his opinion so much. He's clearly got no judgment, or he wouldn't have let you go.'

For a moment, we gazed at each other in astonishment, each taking in the implications of what he had just let slip. This was turning out to be quite a morning, and we hadn't even touched the cream.

Hector caved in first, clearing his throat and turning aside to rummage around in the paperwork on his desk. Then I remembered he'd mentioned another prize.

'So what else did I win? I didn't enter any other categories in the show, apart from the carnival.'

'Ah, well, I took the liberty of entering one on your behalf: the *Writers' Weekly* magazine's annual Book Title and Subtitle Competition, using the clever suggestion that you casually dreamed up at your interview: *Eat My Words: The Confessions of an Encyclopaedia Salesman*.'

He passed me a print-out of an email confirming my win and giving details of the prize: a week-long writers' retreat on Ithaca the following spring. I had to read the email several times before I could take it in.

'I can't believe it! I don't deserve this.'

'I think you do. And of course, where better to launch the writing career that May so wanted for you than a small remote Greek island, home to the father of storytelling and all-round extraordinary chap, Homer?'

'Oh, Hector, how can I ever repay you for your kindness!' I honestly did wonder, because he was my boss, not my boyfriend. Perhaps I should just shake his hand in a business-like manner, or kiss him on the cheek, as if he were my favourite uncle.

Before I could decide, Hector took a step towards me, almost treading on my toes. Setting his hands gently but firmly on my shoulders, he locked his green eyes on my blue ones for a moment. Then, in what felt to me like slow motion, he bent down to press his lips against mine in a long, firm kiss. It was not the kiss of a favourite uncle.

For a few blissful moments, we stood embracing as if there was nothing in the world but us, our bodies so close together that I could feel the mobile phone in the front pocket of his jeans. At least, I think it was his mobile phone.

I was just wishing we could stay there for ever when the shop door creaked, and who should walk in, but Billy.

'I reckons you've got a case there for that sexy harassment, girlie, and no mistake,' said Billy, making his way to his usual tearoom table.

'Or a pay rise,' murmured Hector, letting me go. He spun me round by the shoulders and gave me a little shove in the direction of the tearoom. 'Go on, go and do your stuff.'

'So I'm guessing that means I've passed my trial period?' I grinned at Hector over my shoulder as I washed my hands under the cold tap, ready to assume my waitressing duties. I splashed a little water on my flushed face, too, to cool it down.

Hector settled on his stool behind the counter and rolled up his sleeves, ready to get back to typing his latest manuscript.

'Yes, I think you're here to stay.'

I was certain he was right. I had come home.

ACKNOWLEDGMENTS

First of all, I would like to thank my friends and neighbours in the Cotswold village of Hawkesbury Upton for teaching me how fascinating, funny and rewarding English village life can be. The Hawkesbury Horticultural Show, on whose committee I served for thirteen years, deserves a special mention for sparking the idea for this book and for the Sophie Sayers series.

I am also indebted to author and editor friends further afield for their advice and encouragement: Helen Barbour, Jessica Bell, Lucienne Boyce, Alison Jack, David Penny, Belinda Pollard, and Orna Ross.

As this beautiful new edition goes to press, I'd like to thank the wonderful team at Boldwood Books for their expertise, hard work and their faith in me and in Sophie Sayers: Amanda Ridout, Tara Loder, Sue Lamprell, Madeleine Hamey-Thomas, Emily Reader, Jenna Houston, Justinia Baird-Murray, and Nia Beynon

Finally, thank you for reading Sophie's first adventure. She has yet to solve many more mysteries, and I hope you'll want to share in those too.

With very best wishes,
   Debbie Young

MORE FROM DEBBIE YOUNG

We hope you enjoyed reading *Best Murder In Show*. If you did, please leave a review.

If you'd like to gift a copy, this book is also available as an ebook, digital audio download and audiobook CD.

Sign up to Debbie Youngs' mailing list for news, competitions and updates on future books.

https://bit.ly/DebbieYoungNews

The next in the Sophie Sayers Cozy Mystery series, *Murder at the Vicarage*, is available now.

ABOUT THE AUTHOR

Debbie Young is the much-loved author of the Sophie Sayers and St Brides cosy crime mysteries. She lives in a Cotswold village, where she runs the local literary festival, and has worked at Westonbirt School, both of which provide inspiration for her writing.

Visit Debbie's Website: www.authordebbieyoung.com.

facebook.com/AuthorDebbieYoung

instagram.com/debbieyoungauthor

bookbub.com/authors/debbie-young

twitter.com/DebbieYoungBN

Boldwood

Boldwood Books is an award-winning fiction publishing company seeking out the best stories from around the world.

Find out more at www.boldwoodbooks.com

Join our reader community for brilliant books, competitions and offers!

Follow us
@BoldwoodBooks
@BookandTonic

Sign up to our weekly deals newsletter

https://bit.ly/BoldwoodBNewsletter

Poison
& Pens

POISON & PENS IS THE HOME OF
COZY MYSTERIES SO POUR YOURSELF
A CUP OF TEA & GET SLEUTHING!

DISCOVER PAGE-TURNING NOVELS FROM
YOUR FAVOURITE AUTHORS &
MEET NEW FRIENDS

JOIN OUR
FACEBOOK GROUP

BIT.LYPOISONANDPENSFB

SIGN UP TO OUR
NEWSLETTER

BIT.LY/POISONANDPENSNEWS

9 781804 830567